AYRSHIRE IDYLLS

Neil Munro

FrontList Books

Published by FrontList Books.
An imprint of Soft Editions Ltd,
Edinburgh, Scotland.

First published 1912.

ISBN 1-84350-079-5

AYRSHIRE IDYLLS

Neil Munro was born in 1863 in Inverary, Argyll. He followed a career in journalism, working on various Scottish papers including The Greenock Advertiser, The Glasgow News, The Falkirk Herald, and finally the Glasgow Evening News, where he was made chief reporter at the age of only twenty three, and later editor.

He achieved success with his collections of short stories, poetry and historical novels, and by the time of his death in 1930 was widely hailed as the heir to Scott and Stevenson. He is, however, generally best remembered for his humourous works, most notably the tales of *Para Handy*, *Erchie* and *Jimmy Swan*.

Ayrshire Idylls, his second serious collection of short stories, was first published in 1912.

AYRSHIRE IDYLLS

Contents

Ursa Major

At every reputable tavern on the road from Glasgow, Boswell stopped the chaise, professing a humane anxiety about the horses, and while Johnson lurched round the rude, grey, rough-cast houses, peering at them curiously with his single efficient eye, as if they had been kraals or crannogs, his companion drank claret, chucked waiting-maids under the chin, debated points of politics or faith in Scots with strappers, and felt awake within him the joy of being in a country-side where he was as much respected as in Corsica or the Lews. In London he seldom thought of this land of Ayr, and never with any degree of longing; yet once in the bailiwick of Cunningham, and something in the weather, the landscape, or the folk, restored a sense of self-sufficiency and confidence that were never wholly at his command in the Metropolis, however valiantly he cleared his throat and thrust his chest out in the coffee-houses.

He was known, at every stopping-place, to be the son of Auchinleck; in truth, where his identity was not suspected, he dropped a crafty hint to landlady or landlord which immediately ensured a flattering gush of new civility; but the character of his fat companion baffled them.

"Dr. Samuel Johnson," whispered Boswell once or twice, impressively, with an open hand against his nose. "The Englishman who made the Dictionary; the talk of London! Amazing! What a brain!"

"He'd be a d—d sight better makin' sangs," said the irreverent host of the change-house at Dalry. "Any idiot could make a dictionary, and by the bulk o' him, this ane must hae swallowed his," but that was to his wife when Mr. Boswell had departed. "I'll wager Mr. Jamie has the size o' him!" he added, looking at the chaise go lumbering down the brae. "Ye could see by the kyte o' yon one he was English."

There is a certain kind of autumn day in Ayrshire when in parts, to a not too exigent eye, it has a look of England. Something of Surrey is in those lush well-cultivated plains of Cunningham and Kyle; compared with the Hebrides, whence he had just retreated—those islands wholly void of trees, untracked and desert-melancholy—this landscape seemed familiarly benign and opulent to Johnson. The little towns they passed through might be squalid, but the highway led among delicious fields of vivid green where cattle pastured, or by stubble-land on which wrought peasants, singing as they carted home the sheaves. There were English hedges, garrulous English rooks; below Kilwinning he once got a glimpse of red-tiled roofs uprising over sycamores, and they roused an interest in roofs and tiles he had never felt before; they gladdened his eye that had now grown tired of looking upon grey Caledonian slates. But for the absence of oasts, and smocks, and hop-poles, and the presence of wind-warped pines upon a distant eminence, he could beguile himself with the idea that he travelled among southern wolds.

At Eglinton he found himself in a lordly park, planted with giant secular trees, and mentally amended an impression that the sylvan deities had no harbourage in Scotland.

"H'm!" he purled approvingly. "Not so bad at all, sir! Not so bad! Beeches. Oaks. Fallow deer. H'm! Quite creditable! Even an Englishman might here enjoy the soft vicissitudes of pleasure and repose, attended by all that is calculated to delight, and gratified with the most that elegance and taste in rural beauty may command."

He was charmed with the Countess, who was to be their hostess for the evening. She was elderly, but had the nicest sense of his importance. While Boswell gave assiduous attention to a good old Hock, the great man fixed his disconcerting eye upon her ladyship and boomed opinions, articles of faith, emphatic dogmas, in the papal manner so efficacious with Mrs. Thrale. She agreed with him in everything; her principles in Church and State, he found, were singularly sagacious, being, in every particular, his own; and as he took his candle at midnight through the corridor on his way to bed, he remarked to Boswell, "Sir, her ladyship has a grace which I always thought peculiarly fine in a woman—she is a good listener. It is the one virtue which embellishes and strengthens social intercourse. I confess I had not looked to find it in these wilds; 'tis primarily a civic quality and an essential principle in what we justly call urbanity. When we see in the works of Cicero and others, particularly in Quintilian, the care, the trouble, the continued application which went to form the great men and women of antiquity, we are astonished that there are not more of them. Bolingbroke has remarked——"

"Good-night, sir, God blesh you!" said Boswell, fervently, wringing his hand, and disappearing to a couch for which the exertions of the day and the influence of the excellent Hock had made him ready some hours earlier than usual.

The great man sought his own bedchamber, and before engaging in the nightly struggle with his boots, reversed his candle for a moment to secure a better light. He paid no heed to the grease that guttered on the carpet. He had a soothing sense of having spent some profitable hours.

"I think," he said to himself, "I was particularly happy in my allusions to Ariosto."

. . . .

As the chaise was about to set off in the morning, the Countess took the great man's friend aside. "There are two things sadly lacking in your lion," she remarked, "—a sense of humour, and a family. It took me all my time to keep my countenance when he was lecturing me upon how to bring up children. An amazing man, Mr. Boswell, but I never slept a wink last night for a headache!"

Johnson would have appeared to have slept but poorly too, for he dozed in his corner till they reached Dundonald Castle. Perched high on its isolated knoll, it recalled to him some ruined stronghold he had seen in the Isle of Skye, and seemed wholly inharmonious with surroundings tame and pastoral. They got out of the chaise more closely to examine it, and he roared and laughed till the ruins rang at the homely accommodation of the Sovereign whom he playfully called "King Bob," and who had been born, and died there, with some animated hours between.

"It is strange," he remarked, as they resumed their journey, "that nothing architectural in Scotland seems to be more than a century old except those gloomy fortalices, and the shrines of the Middle Ages. I have perceived no ancient dwellings of the common people; no grange or manor, hamlet, thorp, inn or cottage with a roof-tree older than the holly bushes at its gate. Sir, did all Scots of the past reside in caves, except the barons and ecclesiastics?"

Boswell, both chins sunk profoundly in his black cravat, and rosy at the gills, gave a conciliatory chuckle. "Plenty of stones, sir!" he suggested. "As easy to build a new house as to repair an old one."

"Sir," said his companion, whose punctilio of address appeared grotesque to Boswell when they were in Scotland, though somehow natural in the Mitre tavern; "Sir, I surmise the reason is not so flattering to the racial self-esteem, and has some relation to the conveniency of clay and wattle. Where indigence is national and prolonged through centuries, the affections never root with any depth in soil that poorly rewards the travail of the husbandman, and has no charm of actual possession as with the English yeoman. I begin to see why your countrymen have always been great travellers; strictly speaking, they had never any home except the shadow of the feudal keep. The Scottish pine, the first and hardiest of woodland growths, has no tap-root, but a superficial foundation, and is the easiest of all umbrageous things to sever from its native mould."

"By heavens, sir, you are right! You are always right!" said Mr. Boswell, and in the shadow of the chaise he grimaced to himself.

"Nay, sir, not exactly always," said the Doctor, with that precisian firmness which made him a delight at supper parties. "Omniscience is an attribute of the Deity alone, and on more than one occasion in the course of my life I may perhaps have fallen slightly into error."

"Not at all, sir! Not at all!" protested Boswell, with the utmost gravity, and his companion, crossing his hands complacently on his waistcoat, seemed for the first time to be shaken in conviction.

It was late in the afternoon when they came to Auchinleck, for Boswell had a score of plausible excuses to prolong the journey through a region where his family importance had ever more eloquent recognition the nearer they approached to Lugar Water. There were villages to show to Johnson—Tarbolton of the Beltane hill; Mauchline with its machicolated castle walls and crow-step gables; the wreck of Fail, whose friars

> . . . made guid kail
> On Fridays when they fasted,
> And never wanted gear enough,
> So long as their neighbours' lasted;

Montgomery woods; the river Ayr at Ballochmyle, loud-roaring through deep chasms overhung with foliage and moss—these the nominal occasions for innumerable divagations which were in truth more influenced by Boswell's sentimental interest in some scene reminiscent of youthful dalliance, or his vanity to show himself at mansion-houses with the famous lexicographer.

"One thing, sir, I should like to warn you of," he said to Johnson as they drove to the front of what now, with an unconscious lapse into the custom of the country, he called Place Affleck—"My father, as you know, is a Whig and a Presbyterian, and it were well to avoid discussion either on politics or the Church."

"I shall certainly not be disquisitionary on topics disagreeable to a gentleman in whose house I shelter; especially I shall not be so to your father," answered Johnson, with the finest condescension. "Fortunately there are innumerable other themes on which I hope I may consider myself qualified with edification to dilate."

Lord Auchinleck, though only a few years older than his guest, appeared in no way overawed by a visitation so momentous; on the contrary, he looked with a depreciatory eye and a grim pursed mouth of disapproval on the corpulent gentleman who had been taking James away from business, and who now rolled ox-like through the hall, already booming erudite opinions upon Scottish weather.

As he disappeared upstairs to repair his toilet, his hosts uneasily regarded one another.

"I wonder if he has his tawse with him?" said

Lord Auchinleck. "I think sometimes, Jamie, ye're gane gyte! First it was yon land-loupin' Corsican Paoli ye were traikin' after, and now it's ower the hills ayont Dunblane wi' this auld dominie that keepit a schule and ca'd it an academy. Your frien', I can see already, is just a hectorin', conceited schulemaister, still drum-majorin' bairns."

And in spite of Mr. Boswell's warning, the altercation came to pass. Five days' incessant rain, which amply justified the stranger's estimate of Scottish weather, held him prisoner in the house among the classic folios of Auchinleck. His ponderous figure seemed, to the eyes of his host, to swell and make the library smaller every day, as if he got unhallowed sustenance there between the common meals, a flatulent vampire diet from the mildewed tomes. There was a blink of sunshine on the Sabbath and the Boswells went to the kirk, but lofty Anglican disdain for what he called a chapel made the Doctor stay at home. Magnificently and immovably disposed in an easy-chair, over the edge of which his ampler parts seemed to roll like something viscous, he surveyed mankind from China to Peru, set everybody right on everything and boomed—and boomed—and boomed. Lord Auchinleck, no trivial dialectician, and a man who had seen the world, not through the smoke of a coffee-room or the skylight window of an attic in Bolt Court, was early worsted in the fray, with a voice incapable of shouting down a man, as he said despairingly, "that has been bellowin' a' his days, and would keep up practice on a grosset bush if he couldna get a human audience." That the onerous task of entertaining such a guest should be shared by somebody, he invited guests to dinner; Dr. Johnson found in one of them, the minister, Mr. Dun, a sounding-board for loud prelections on the Druids, the Chaldeans, Gymnosophists of Ethiopia, Turditanes of Spain, Augurs of Rome, Apollo's priests in Greece, Phoebades and Pythonissae, their oracles and phantasms, but above all others that iniquitous high priest of Rome.

" 'Twixt Roman pope and English prelacy I never could see a chink ye could stick a knife in," said Lord Auchinleck abruptly, and the fat was in the fire.

The war-horse snorted and let out a couple of buttons. *"Dum vitant stulti vitia in contraria currunt,"* he retorted. "When fools avoid one vice they run into another of an opposite character, and your Covenanters in their zeal to abolish ritual have abolished beauty."

"The graves of Peden and Cameron are there on the hills behind us, sir!" cried Auchinleck; "and their death was beauteous as the rose."

"The Presbyterian Church, sir, has not produced by the hands of its divines a single work of letters," said Johnson.

"It is plain, sir, you have not read Durham on Galatians," retorted Auchinleck.

"I have not, sir," answered Johnson. "Have you?" and got his answer in Lord Auchinleck's confusion. "I should as soon read Cromwell on Terpsichore."

"Praise God for Cromwell!" cried his lordship.

"What good did Cromwell ever do?" Dr. Johnson asked.

"I'll tell ye that, man," answered Auchinleck. "He gart kings ken they had a lith in their necks. Pass up the bottle, James, and we'll drink to the confusion of all Jacobites."

. . . .

The post-chaise started off for Edinburgh in the morning. "There's nae cure for the disease o' bein' a dominie," said Lord Auchinleck to his son as they watched the servants packing the baggage. "Your wife is right to be vexed at seein' ye dance at the end of a string in the hands o' yon big bear. Call yersel' a Boswell! It was wiser-like ye were attendin' to your proper business."

James Boswell chuckled, gave a wink implying superhuman subtlety, and replied, "That's all right, papa; he's really a splendid fellow if you once get used to him, and I see my way to make him into a book."

"A book!" cried Auchinleck. "Leviathan on a hook! The man's a giant, Jamie, and you're but a wee bit dwarf."

"Just so, papa," said Boswell, "but a dwarf on the shoulders of a giant can see a good deal farther than the giant. Believe me, papa, he'll make a splendid book!"

Mossgiel Rab

Gilbert, in his shirt sleeves, read a book—*The Life of Hannibal*—more to improve that douce mind of his than for amusement, seemingly, since he yawned at the turning of every page; and Blane, the ploughboy, mended harness. A north wind whooped in the spacious chimney, where a pot hung boiling low on the swee, and the trees, that sheltered Mossgiel steading, cried piteously as for entrance, rapping at the white-harled gable.

On such nights, Gilbert's brother felt, more poignantly than usual, his passion for the wild, his fierce impatience with the humdrum tenor of their peasant home. It was the fire that mainly lit the kitchen; a tallow candle guttering on the brace but gave to the wholesome glow of peat a wan complexion, a hint of the artificial, and to the poet a discontented thought of other chambers read about or seen through unshuttered windows momentarily, where numberless candles shone against sconces on the walls of the well-to-do. He cast a curious glance about him as he sat in a swither with his fingers on the laces of his shoes—at the low, stained rafters, the planked enclosures of the beds, the dresser of chipped blue delf, the sleeping collie, the bubbling pot, the studious brother, the industrious Blane; and the thought in his bosom came to his lips with no restraining—"Gibbie! is this—is this, can ye tell me, our eternal doom?"

Gilbert straightened his stooped back, and turned his fire-freckled face on Robert.

"What's the time?" said he.

Burns drew a watch from the fob of his breeches, glanced at the dial, snapped the words "half-nine," and strode to the pot that swung on the chimney chain. He lifted the lid, peered at the contents—to-morrow's dinner—and shut them from his view again with an iron clatter.

"Offal!" said he. "Is that Hannibal yet ye're at? Was he fed, Gibbie, do ye think, on offal?"

"I would ca' nae guid meat offal, Rab," said Gilbert. "And if it had been offal at Capua it wad hae been better for Hannibal and his men. Half-nine? It's time we were bedded."

The eyes of Burns fired deeply under their cliff of brow, the flambeaux of revolt; he grimaced and shrugged his shoulders. "Half-nine," said he, "and bed! What's in the veins o' ye, Gib?—is't buttermilk? In mine, thank God! it's blood. I'm for nae stupor on a caff mattress in a loft at half-nine on a nicht like this so lang's there's men to be met at Poosie Nancy's. Here's you and General Hannibal, every line of him wide awake and thrang wi' tramping sodgers, and ye're ganting for your bed; and here's Jock Blane cobbling brechams, content himsel' in the trams o' the dung-cart o' destiny—a kind o' patient cuddy! Please yersels, but I'm neither for bed nor brechams! Three-score years and ten's the allotted span; I misdoubt I'll see but the half o't, and six-and-twenty's gane. The lave o' my years are no' that lang that I'm ready to gae to bed at nine and lie like an auld maid chitterin' and listenin' to the win'—do ye hear't, Gibbie? Do ye hear't, Jock? It's got the deil's own spite at puir Mossgiel, and we're in a bit box, buried under snaw, three nameless bodies, and twa wi' the disease o' dull contentment. As for me, I'm choking, and I'm aff to Mauchline!"

He threw a plaid about him, scrugged down his bonnet on his brow, and made for the door.

"Poosie Nancy's, I suppose?" said Gilbert. "It's no' the best o' company ye'll get there."

"At least," said Burns, "they're no ganting for their beds or cloutin' brechams for their ain necks, and they'll no' be buried before their time!" and he slammed the door behind him.

"Faith! he's in a droll key, Rab, the nicht," said Blane, the ploughboy.

"It's pride," said Gilbert helplessly; "fair upsettin' vanity! Wealth's the warld's curse! He's awa' wi' his half-year's pay in his pouches—three pun' ten!"

. . . .

Mossgiel lay high on the breast of the brae and Burns for a moment stood at the door of it to look on Kyle below him, blanched to a cold reclusive beauty by the snow. The sky was held by racing clouds, and the moon, at the full, fell giddily from space through the hurrying vapours, chased as in terror by her sweet young infant stars. Old trees overhung the dwelling, the tall haw-bushes made a hedge to shelter it; among them went the wind, that seemed to sweep the shire of Ayr of all its chilly elements and pile them, drift-white, in the wide quadrangle of the steading. Some sparks from the fire that Blane was banking for the night came up through the low chimney, and lived a moment—red, aspiring little stars, that gave to the poet a fancy of his own and all men's sad futility; his heart played thud in his breast and he gasped with an emotion such as poets feel from things that may seem trivial to the world, but to the gifted have the import of a cataclysm. There was some spirit in the scene and hour—cold, pure, austere, remonstrant—that made him swither on the threshold, for he knew already that in the tavern he would find no higher uplift to his soul than came this moment from communion with the cleansed night. But still—but still, the sober face of the virtuous Gilbert ready for sleep, and the silence of the assiduous Blane, came back to him, and the sordid pot of tripe and thairm, and the dreary prospect of those waukrife hours in bed, with all his thoughts insurgent against slumber, and by comparison the barmy smells of Poosie Nancy's tavern, the feel of a pewter can, the gluck of poured ale, the loud dispute of hinds, and the admiration for his gifts of wit and clinking song-stuff, proffered an alternative that could not be resisted. He summoned the memory of other carousing nights to his weakening inclination for the ploy; stepped over the frozen duck-dub in the lane, and down between the mantled fields to the lighted village.

Upon these boozing peasants he made, in

truth, but a rare intrusion. They felt half pleased and half disquieted, for though his presence was a kind of compliment, they had the start of him by several chappins, and they knew him for a man too apt to keep the crack on a level above the long-continued stretch of their ale-mused brains. His was the table-head, the fir-wood lug-chair; his the next round, his as many rounds as he cared to pay for; and the room of Poosie Nancy rang with a Bacchic symphony.

Before him, for a little, snow-white Kyle, the surging cloud and the moon intruded; in pauses of the trumpery conversation came across his mind that glance to the heart of things, that second's ecstasy he had found before the house on the brae, so that he almost rued the disposition that had brought him among this noisy crew. But one man had a story—not for parlours, witty, human, wicked, rich with the arterial blood of passion and grotesque of circumstance such as men heard then in Ayrshire even between the kirks; and another had a novel air with a ranting and resistless chorus, and the moon—the calm, clean, sovran moon—went down behind the clouds of vile tobacco; and over the remembered vision of the pure white fields was a mantle drawn, and the sound of the wind in the trees around Mossgiel was drowned in foolish chatter.

And yet he sought, as he sat among it, for those revelations of his loftier self; he drank with a deliberate purpose—not wholly for the warm sense of equality with these, his fellow-victims in the joke of Fate; for that rare elation, that confidence, that content, of which at times he had found the barley-fields possessed the magic key. Once he found it—in a thought that tore him from his company, a thought that only briefly kept a concrete form in the brain of him, then broke in a thousand iridescent pieces, each as precious as the whole, never to be brought together into something rational—a joyous, heady gambol through centuries of sun and storm; song, women, and the old lost fields of the youth he had never properly known; a sense of warmth, well-being and perfection.

They had sung, among them, these dear hinds, his brothers, whom so well he understood, and pitied, one of his own songs, and this was his happy hour! A fiddle jigged in his brain, and Poosie Nancy's reeking chamber was transfigured.

Only for a space. The hour was late, right well had they scourged the gantrys for their ale; the morning hurried towards the fields of Ayr, and a woman stood beseeching for her husband, or his wages, at the door.

The man, the very boon companion who had started Burns's song, hung his head, and the shrill high voice of the vintner could be heard behind the wife's pathetic figure, proclaiming the respectability of her house, and her helplessness to quench the drouth of any man with the fate to belong to Tarbolton.

"Vive la bagatelle! hae ye no' the money, Will?" said Robert Burns; and the man said, "No' a doit!"

"That's bad!" said Burns, with his fingers combing back the dank black locks from his burning brow; "ay, man, that's damn bad! If I was a married man"—he laughed a little bitterly—"if I was a married man, I would likely still be Rabbie Burns; here, wife, it's a' that's left; it's aff-and-on thirty shillings; your man's a bonny singer, and I'm for hame."

. . . .

It was dawn when he came to the farm-house door, and Blane, the ploughboy, beat his arms across his breast ere he turned to mucking the byre. Kyle fell away below in billows of grey, and the cocks were crowing. The smoke of a green fire floated from the chimney-head, and the countenance of Gilbert, blameful and questioning, filled the door of the trance.

"Ye've had a nicht of it, Rab!" said he.

"I've had that, Gib!" said his brother, peaceably.

"And what did it cost ye?" asked the keeper of the frugal conscience of Mossgiel.

"It cost me exactly three pun' ten, and cheap at the money," said the poet.

"On drink!" said Gilbert, horrified.

"Sae be't!" said Robert; "whether or no', I'll get the name o't."

The Lion of the Covenant

The morning broke upon the country with a threat of heat. To the east the moorland stretched, a shoreless sea of mist with dim conjectural isles of planted firs; to the north a darker haze that might hold thunder hung over Wealth o' Waters. No breath of air was stirring in the trees round Meadowhead; the Ayr went on its way to sea, repining; doves crooned about the steading.

Hackston had gone forth before the sun was up and "smelled the morning," as his phrase was for a reconnaissance; with owl-like vigilance he was often out for hours in the mirk of night while the others slept, scouring the fields and byways, sniffing about the outskirts of a hamlet or steading with a cocked ear and every sense alert for signs of circumspection like his own. The night-walker! What thoughts, fantastic, and of the early savage unlit world, attended him in these nocturnal sallies! He brought back with him into the daylight, airs of a double life—of secret knowledge gained, of wicked intimacy, strange surmise.

This morning, having scanned the country, he returned with speed to Mitchell's barn. His fellows lay asleep, lifeless as lichened stones, wrapped up in their shepherd plaids and their weapons by them. From the open door of the byre across the steading square he could hear quiet voices of the lassies milking, and the purr of milk fall in their pails. He swithered to rouse the men, to change that blissful trance for consciousness of perils that encompassed; to hurry them out again on the old vexed hunted ways. But no time must be lost if Mitchell's barn was not to be a slaughter-house before the milk that now was frothing in the cogues was cold.

He bent and caught the hand of Cameron firmly, saying nothing—so had they learned to wake each other without alarm, and Cameron sat up among the hay with his eyes wide open and his hand upon his sword. He looked grotesquely out of place in such a situation, with hay in his dishevelled hair and his cravat reduced to the condition of a dish-clout; slight of stature, girlish pink in the complexion, fair curls upon his temples, a touch of the Dutch cleric in his attire.

"What is't ?" said he in a whisper.

"Only the old story," Hackston muttered, taking in his belt another hole. "I have been out since three, and searching round by Mauchline and Auchmillan. No sign of them was there, but over near to Catrine House I saw a smoke among the trees. Ayont the policies I came on a hundred-and-twenty tethered horse and the holsters on them. It's Bruce of Earlshall; I learned from a laddie in the fields that they ken our hiding; already they may be on the road."

Cameron took these tidings calmly. "I had it on my mind last night that something was portending," he remarked, and got upon his feet. "The evening was unco quiet, like one that brooded something soon to burst upon us, and we were far too merry for men in gear of war. Ah, Rathillet, I do not like to be light of heart! The jaunty mood aye boded ill for me. We must rouse the lads."

He looked at his companions stretched upon the hay in all death's uncouth attitudes. "Poor lads!" said he, as one who stood outside their weariness; and again "Poor lads! I'm sweir to break their sleep! It has come with me, Rathillet, to a point of conscience. I would not wonder if my Hour has come."

A little short of sight, and still be-rheumed with sleep, he lifted up his eyes and blinked at Hackston, a tall dark, shaggy man who had a scar upon his brow.

"The Hour," said Hackston with a gesture of impatience, "is no more to be foretold than next week's weather. Listen! By the grace o' God the mornin's fine and misty; till it's close on noon ye'll no' can see the other side o' an acre park. It's for you to quit us here and make your way by Highburn o' Need to Avonhead and down on Straven. You daurna take a horse; ye'll have to shank it; Michael 'll gang wi' ye."

"But you?—and them?" said Cameron, indicating those who slept.

"We'll move up the river by the Wellwood, or Muirkirk, work round the back o' Cairntable, and through the hills to Sanquhar. At the worst of it we'll have drawn them off your track, though they may overtake us; but there's a chance, forbye, that the weather may break down. Give me Ayrs Moss in steep wi' water and I'll defy all Earlshall's horse!"

Cameron pondered but a moment. "No," said he with firmness, "rather will I die warm death with men, than skulk with timid bestial. And Sanquhar, say you? It may well be Sanquhar, Rathillet! Were it not for yon night in Sanquhar, there werena fifty hundred merks on Richie Cameron's head. . . . Michael! Michael!"

His brother's name rang through the barn, and Michael with a leap was on his feet.

"Are they there?" he asked upon the instant of his waking, like a man that had been dreaming terrors.

"There, 'faith, are they!" answered Hackston; "at any rate they're at Catrine, too close for our comfort, and it's time we put the muir below our feet."

Three score of men were in the hay; they rose, like Michael, at the shout of Richard Cameron, and buckled on their graith with what might seem composure, and the milking was not done when they were gathered on the causey of the yard with twenty horse. Urged by the farmer's wife and her servant-girls, they drank milk and put some bannocks newly off the girdle in their pockets, but not till Cameron had sanctified the day with prayer: "Oh feed thy people with thy rod, the flock of thine heritage, which dwell solitarily in the wood, in the midst of Carmel: let them feed in Bashan and Gilead, as in the days of old," he supplicated in the words of Micah. They stood, unbonneted about him, their hands in their shabble hilts, and he appeared as one peculiarly uplifted by communion with transcendent things. His countenance seemed lit with inner light, so wan it was, so ardent, quivering with emotion—some deep conviction, secret joy. His voice had a curious and unusual quality; youth's timbre was departed from it; while it might be nothing but the morning haar that gave it this unwonted body, it appeared to them miraculously full and rich, Mosaic in authority.

Finally he bathed his face and hands in water brought at his request by one of the women, and dried them, saying, "This is their last washing; I have need to make them clean, for there are many to see them."

"Then you will not take my counsel and leave us now?" asked Hackston in a last appeal. "Scotland needs you, and you are a man of peace."

"It may be that I was not come to send peace, but a sword," said Cameron, simply. "And I have something more than an inkling that my Hour is come."

He got upon his horse. Michael and Hackston rode on his either side. The little squadron, broken into guards for rear and van, moved eastward at a walking pace with the footmen in the centre.

There never surely was a day more eerie out of winter; high though the sun must be in heaven, there prevailed about them a peculiar gloaming as they marched between the woods of Sorn. It seemed as if the night had tangled with the trees and could not yet withdraw itself, and out upon the open country fog was thick upon the laboured fields. Vague forms uprose like skerries through the rack of leaden seas, the loom of cliffs, of thickets, or of moving bestial; sounds, muffled to the rumour of conspiracy, came from below where Ayr ran coiling through the bouldered flats, or, even more disquieting, the chatter of strange birds, or owls lamenting in their usual hours of sleep. A cloying scent of meadow-sweet was in the fainting air. As they marched across the country, they might well appear, even to themselves, a disembodied band astray in space and time; phantoms perhaps of ancient vanquished men from stricken fields of Shiloh, of Ephraim or Flodden.

No word was passed between them for a while as they went through this singular morning mist, and they were on the ridge of the rise at Merkland, when for the first time Hackston spoke.

"I never saw a day like this in July month; or surely I am fey!" quo' he. "It fairly dauntens me!"

"An unco morn, in faith!" said Michael Cameron, and looked at his brother's face—the wee wan face beside his shoulder, lifted to the east and settled in a smiling ecstasy.

"What ails ye, Richard?" he inquired with apprehension. "Have ye a glint o' onything? Say, Richard, have ye seen——? Oh, Richard, is there something?"

He whom the brother questioned, as one that spoke from a great distance, lifted up his voice and said, "The Hour is at hand; I see the mist break and I hear far off the sound of horsemen."

They stopped, stricken, in a cluster round about him, men and horses mingled, and they strained their ears to listen for the beat of hooves.

No sound of any kind was to be heard except the river muttering and the lapwing's call.

"I misdoubt, sir, you are mistaken," at the last said Hackston, but in truth he doubted not at all and his face was like the sleet. Yet still he would maintain the show of doubt if only to give heart and hope a little more to these poor wanderers. "There never was a day in some particulars more to my taste," he added. "They will be hard put to it to get a glisk o' us, and I winna wonder but they're on the road to Galston."

Again spake their shepherd as from a distant place, saying, "I see the mist break and hear the sound of horsemen. Ere this hour pass ye shall likewise hear and see, even as I hear and see." He looked over his shoulder towards Cumnock, and then, turning to the east, held out his arms and said: "I have glorified Thee on earth; I have finished the work which Thou gavest me to do. And now, O Father, glorify Thou me with Thine own self with the glory which I had with Thee before the world was. I have manifested Thy name unto the men which Thou gavest me out of the world: Thine they were, and Thou gavest them me; and they have kept Thy word. And now I am no more in the world, but these are in the world, and I come to Thee, Holy Father; keep through Thine own name those whom Thou hast given me, that they may be one, as we are."

"Richard! Richard!" cried his brother Michael in his ear, like one that summoned at the yetts of death, and the other looked at him with a yearning aspect, brimming with affection, and put an arm upon his arm, but nothing said.

Hardly had their ranks re-formed than a little flaff of purging wind came out of the west and a few small drops of rain. Hackston bade them halt, and in behind the ridge they watched the mist roll off the country like a hodden blanket. It lay upon the moss-land longer than elsewhere, and while as yet the muir in their propinquity was still enveloped, every feature of the shire beyond it to the south was plainly visible. They searched it with their eyes as Moses searched from Pisgah, yet for no promised Gilead or utmost sea, but for some import of the thing they feared, and down by Lugar they saw peesweeps of a sudden rise in a cloud and wheel.

"My God, they're yonder!" Hackston cried. The startled birds were screaming over a vedette whose mounted form was clear upon the sky-line.

"They have gone round by Cumnock to cut us off!" said Michael, in a voice dejected.

A fierce vexation shook the hunted men, and he alone who was their shepherd heretofore but now was passed, remained apart with gaze averted, litten up with spiritual loveliness, the countenance of one beatified. So bask the ones elected, with the morning on their foreheads.

Hackston scrutinised the sky, and "Think ye it will thunder, Michael?" he inquired. "It is unco black upon the hill."

"What odds?" said Michael, looping the naked shabble on his wrist.

"Now would I give twenty years of life ordained to me for an hour of blashing rain," said Hackston. "There's nothing but the Moss for it!"

"The Moss!" exclaimed his company.

"The same! Wi' hard ground and Earlshall's horse we wouldna bide the stour o' a single charge; wi' the Moss a swamp and us well posted, they have, wi' a' their horse, no great advantage. Is it not so, sir?"

Their umquhile shepherd for a moment made no answer; combing his horse's mane through idle fingers.

Then he spoke, saying, "Jacob to the spoil and Israel to the robbers, but my power is made perfect through weakness. Tarry ye here and I alone will go to them and deliver myself to their hands."

He gathered up his reins, and made to leave the others, airting to the region whence his searchers were to come, but at a sign from Hackston, Michael barred his way.

"Nay! nay!" cried Hackston with authority. "For yon way stands the gibbet, and your head upon a stick above the Netherbow."

"But this poor head may satisfy; it is worth five thousand pieces of silver."

"If heads they want, then," Hackston answered roughly, "they maun buy them by the score; we will not break the parcel. And better for us to perish in the rashes now than live a little longer just to girn upon a fir-stob at the hinder-end. It's at the close o' day we best like some companionship."

They left the road, went down upon the riverside, and crossed it at the Tarraoch ford; then out upon the Moss where Hackston saw a knoll that promised some security against a sudden overwhelming charge of horse. About them, when they halted, lay green bogs, long heather tufts, and hag-holes inky-dark with peaty water. Enormous clouds, pit-black, were banking up behind them; Cairntable rumbled, and there fell some heavier drops of heated rain. The muir, that had been covered up with vapours as with wool, was now swept clear of these ambiguous elements, displayed itself a desert plain most melancholy, whereon the harshest vegetation grew and humankind had never made a track. A trotting squadron moved upon its southern verge.

The Covenanters cast their plaids, scrugged down their bonnets on their foreheads, looked to the priming of their pistols—few of them had muskets—tossed aside the scabbards of their swords. For the main part tenant bodies better used to wield the flail than flourish lethal weapons, they were ignorant of sergeant drill and awkward in such movements as demanded combination; they huddled like a herd of sheep at first and Hackston broke them out in ranks. The horsemen he divided, posting them upon the flanks.

No sooner was he done than thunder crashed above them and the rain descended in a blinding sheet. He groaned with deep vexation, "Ah! had it only come a kenning sooner, we would have them plunging to the houghs!"

"Look at him!" said Michael, pointing to his brother.

He had come off his horse and stood beside its head, contemplating the ground. And as they moved to urge him to the saddle, he upheld his brow from which some private glee had taken every wrinkle; looked over and beyond the coming enemy, and began to pray. He prayed like one exalted, while the rain threshed on his face, commending them to God as creatures summoned on a desperate trial; so having done, he turned to his brother Michael saying, "This is the day that I have longed for, and the death that I would choose to die, fighting against our dear Lord's enemies avowed."

And now the enemy was nigh at hand—a troop of Airlie's sabres with dragoons of Strachan's; Earlshall at their head upon a sorrel charger. They plashed across the Moss in broken order to avoid the haggs; no sound came from them but the clink of harness, and that seemed like the chirp of crickets in the swoons of silence in between the thunder-peals. The mountain hare arose before them, scudding through the puddles; the whaup gave out her doleful whistle. Far to the east and north the hills were roaring, and each glen had its particular desolation.

At less than bow-shot Bruce drew up his following and threw out a score of horse. They started at a canter for the flanks of Hackston's company, picking out the rush-tufts for securer footing, skirting holes, indifferent to formation. The voice of Hackston, shouting some command, was drowned in an appalling burst of thunder so contiguous it seemed to shake the air and rock the earth's foundations. Two of the dragoons slid off their horses clumsily; it looked at first as if they had been lightning-smitten, but they had been shot; the smoke of muskets drifted for a moment, sulphurous and acrid, round the knoll. The Covenanters stood, as it appeared, within the very core of nature's agony; peal followed peal; the lightning venomously stabbed and water fell as if some universal cistern had burst. There was seen in His temple the ark of His testament, and all things were afraid.

With frantic plunge the frightened horses upon Hackston's flanks broke from the ranks in wild disorder, quitted the solid mound and separately dashed into the green morass, whence streamed upon them like a spate, and on the clustered footmen on the mound, the ordered mass of Bruce's cavalry. Their carbines rattled and their sabres sheared. No quailing was among the Covenanters; each one, severed from his fellows, and surrounded, fought if it were upon his very knees, but all was purposeless, deranged, and random; each for himself and all authority dispelled.

Hackston, roaring, cut his way through the dragoons to lose his horse upon the farther side; he turned to find himself confronted by an old acquaintance who thrust at him with malignant fury; Ramsay he beat off, but was himself cut down behind, stripped of his weapons, bound—to have his members scattered through the towns a fortnight later.

For a little Richard Cameron and his brother fought together side by side, upon their feet, the persecutors sure of them but sweir to mar them for the Grassmarket. The brothers heartened one another with repeated cries—old Scripture slogans of the days of tribulation; lent each other hands and eyes, and seemed at last to their infuriate foes miraculously endowed.

The first to fall was Michael, sabre-cleft. He heaved upon his side, and grabbled vainly at the heather in a vain attempt to pluck himself from out the deeps of death, then lifted up his hands and pointed to the gurly sky, in which a casement opened.

"Farewell, Michael, I'll keep tryst," cried Richard and was swept before a squad of the dragoons.

The horses rode him down and trampled over him, but he arose like one unharmed, and still the claymore knotted to his wrist, to find himself before the levelled barrels of a file of Strachan's horse.

For a moment he stood smiling as if ravished by some vision of delight, his look not of this yird but of a land delectable, no more a creature but a spirit sanctified; then, spreading out his arms, walked calmly to the guns.

"Neither by an Army nor Strength, but by My spirit, said the Lord of Hosts!" he cried, and fell face-downward as the horsemen fired.

Burns and Clarinda

The light of the afternoon came flooding through the windows; bathed Miss Nimmo's parlour in a golden radiance, and gave a mellow, pensive tone even to the poet's reverie. He sat with his face in the shadow, for he had not yet got rid of his rustic fears of these fine Edinburgh ladies, the very elegance of whose apartments contributed to his uneasiness. With any man living he could hold his own, but these unusual women—calm, confident, unabashed before the fervour of his eye; moving like swans, conversing like schoolmasters upon abstract things, witty, prone to mocking smiles—they were the very devil! He feared yet he adored them, since they had for him abundantly the one thing dear to poets and lovers—Mystery.

"A penny for your thoughts, Mr. Burns," said the charming Mrs. Maclehose, showing her drift-white teeth in a smile that seven or eight years ago had done terrific execution among the bucks at Edinburgh balls.

"A poet's thoughts are surely worth more than that, Nancy," said Miss Nimmo.

"It all depends," said Mrs. Maclehose archly; "he might be thinking us very uninteresting after meeting such sublime examples of our sex as the Duchess of Gordon."

"A fine woman!" said Burns with some

enthusiasm. “In her company I forget that she’s a duchess and feel myself a duke.”

“It’ll likely be her awccent,” drawled Mrs. Maclehose, in a clever imitation of the Duchess’s uncompromising Scots, and the charming mimic fell a little in his estimation; he liked his women, above all things, kind.

“It’s an accent that some of the greatest in the land have respected from the lips of the Duchess of Gordon,” said Burns, with a curious tension of the jaw and a flash of the eyes. “I’m a Scot myself.”

“The very greatest!” said Mrs. Maclehose, grasping the generous widths of her gown and dropping him a courtesy, half ironic.

She was a lovely woman, Mrs. Maclehose, and Burns, with the sense of sex as keen as his poetic vision, regarded her in this playful mood with his old illusion that here might be the long-desired Ideal—the woman of whom one could never weary. She was short in stature, just the right height for the head to fit in the nook of his shoulder; with hands and feet small and delicate; fair complexion; flushed with health, with dancing eyes and a soft vivacious utterance. An air of elegance, refinement, grace, seemed to respire from her presence, and she could rise like a bird, and instantly, to the loftiest, most poetic fancy he cared to express. They did not breed that kind of woman in the shire of Ayr; at all events, he had never had the chance to meet them.

And she admired him—that with Burns, as with all sons of art, was the main thing! He knew she did, and what was better still, he knew it was not wholly for his poetry, of which she generally preferred what shrewder judgment would have told her were the poorest stanzas. She admired him for his fame and for his story, and most of all she plainly admired him as a Man. So far as women were concerned, the poet would sooner be loved for his legs than for his lyrics.

She admired him so much that he would have been quite at his ease with her, were it not for the presence of their hostess, Miss Nimmo, who too obviously realised the situation, and was amused at something.

"What are you smiling at?" asked Burns, when the visitor was gone in a rustle of silk, leaving a wake of lavender perfume, and for the poet a sense of deprivation. Miss Nimmo had come from the door with that sly and merry aspect which women assume when they mean to betray the weaknesses or follies of their sex.

"Nancy has asked me to take you to a dish of tea at her house on Thursday," she replied primly.

"I'll go!" said Burns emphatically.

"Of course, of course!" said the quiet little lady; "I kent you would go, and I said as much. Nancy's raptures were surely not to be altogether thrown away on you! You must be the proud man to excite such sudden adoration in our impressionable sex."

"A fine woman!" said Burns fervently.

"H'm! So's the Duchess of Gordon," was the reply of Miss Nimmo. "Do you know, I think, so far as women are concerned, you're gey and easy pleased," and she smiled up at him with her shrewd, pawky, plain little face, sadly disconcerting him, for he was not used to the subtleties of women who knew the game.

"What do you mean?" he asked suspiciously.

"I was thinking," said the old lady, "of a girl called Jean Armour," and she looked at him with penetrating and unflinching eyes.

"Easy pleased," said he, with a flush appearing on his pallid countenance. "Madam, if you knew Jean Armour——"

"My rural swain," said the lady, rapping him on the fingers with her fan, "you'll maybe can write braw poetry, but there are things you do not understand. When I talked about your being easily pleased, I was not passing judgment on the girl I name, whom I have never had the honour to see, but thinking of what is due to her, and of the way that you forget, and of your readiness to interest yourself in any other bonny face that comes the way. It's wonderful to me, who ken women, how you clever men can be glamoured by a little flattery from any designing creature with a languishing eye——"

"You are hardly fair to your friend or loyal to your sex," said the poet, relieved and laughing.

"I like my friend in spite of her failings," said Miss Nimmo, taking snuff. "I have plenty of my own; and she was made by nature for the beguiling of silly men-bodies like yourself. And I am so loyal to my sex that I cannot think but with compassion of the lassie Jean, in Ayr."

"I can think of her mysel'," said Burns,

abruptly and uneasily. “I hope you haven’t mentioned her to Mrs. Maclehose?”

“It wouldna make muckle odds if I did—to Mrs. Maclehose.”

“Who is she? What is she?” eagerly pursued the poet.

“An honest married woman who has had a family of four,” replied Miss Nimmo, with a faint malicious smile, and the face of the poet fell a little—a family of four was something of a staggerer!

“A widow?” he asked indifferently, remembering there had been no mention of a Mr. Maclehose.

“In a fashion,” said Miss Nimmo. “Grass. Her husband is in the Indies, and she hopes he’ll bide there. Meantime it is plain she wants to keep herself in practice at the gallivanting. I’m touched at her raptures over your book; she must have raced through it unco fast, for she borrowed my copy at nine o’clock last night when she heard there was a chance she might see you here.”

“She’s clever enough to understand even my poor book at a gallop,” said Burns, pulling down his embroidered waistcoat. “What time did you say was her tea?”

Miss Nimmo sighed. “Hech, sirs! and this is genius!” said she. “My Nancy’s got a head like a fizzy drink, and a tongue like the clatter-bane o’ a duck, and the Bard o’ Caledon, forgettin’ the ‘true pathos and sublime’ he writes so bonnily about, is just as easily made dizzy wi’ her arts as if he were a writer’s clerk. Ye read French?”

"Yes," said the bard; and she plucked a volume from the table and directed his attention to Voltaire's counsel to the Duchess of Richelieu :—

> Ne vous aimez pas trop; c'est moi qui vous en prie,
> C'est le plus sûr moyen de vous aimer toujours.
> Il faut mieux être amis tout le temps de la vie
> Que d'être amants pour quelques jours.

"Quite so!" said the poet; "it's long since I learned that philosophy for mysel', but what o'clock did ye say was the lady's tea?"

. . . .

An injured knee kept Burns to his lodgings for some days after this, and he missed the chance of drinking tea with Mrs. Maclehose, on whose charms of person and mind he had the better opportunity for musing. One evening, after a succession of blythe and roystering visitors, in a state of pleasant exaltation he wrote the lady a letter, drafting it carefully first in the very best style of "The Elegant Letter Writer," on which he and Gilbert had one time modelled their correspondence.

> I do love you, if possible, still better for having so fine a taste and turn in poesy (he wrote). I have again gone wrong in my usual unguarded way, but you may erase the word, and put esteem, respect, or any other tame Dutch expression you please in its place. I believe there is no holding converse or carrying on correspondence with an amiable woman—much less a GLORIOUSLY AMIABLE FINE WOMAN, without some mixture of that delicious passion

whose most devoted slave I have more than once had the honour of being.

"That's the style for Mistress Bluestocking!" he exclaimed complacently, as he read it over. "It wouldna be muckle use wi' Jean," and then, resuming his pen, he wrote these memorable words :—

> Oh Clarinda! shall we not meet in a state, some yet unknown state of being where the lavish hand of plenty shall minister to the highest wish of benevolence, and where the chill north wind of prudence shall never blow over the flowery fields of enjoyment! If we do not, man is made in vain.

"By the Lord!" said he, "that's genius!" and taking another toddy went well pleased with himself to bed.

Next morning he read the still-unposted letter, and laughed. "Oh, Robin! Robin! whatna Machiavelli!" he exclaimed. "And whatna dulcet key! 'Lavish hand of plenty,' by Gad! 'North wind of prudence'! 'Flowery fields of enjoyment'! Keep us! what transparent sophistry! It would make even Jean laugh, and Miss Nimmo, if she saw it, would be unco nippy. Oh, Rab! ye write a bonny letter!"

He took a penny from his pocket and tossed it.

"Heads," said he when it fell. "The letter goes, with north winds and flowery fields and a' the rest o't; I wouldna say but it's just the thing for Nancy Maclehose."

And so began the Clarinda correspondence.

The Cloak of Darkness

On the morning of the murder at Priesthill, a figure wrapped to the heel in black came out from the woods of Sorn—dark groves of refuge, fear, and spiritual ambush; sped westward by the rough bush-cumbered little valley where the water of the Ayr went splashing, and nowhere ventured on the highway which pursued the moorland level. Below his tricorne hat there showed grey haffits blowing in the wind, and a velvet mask which gave alarming import to his movements, that were stealthy, sly, and calculated, as of one who was on paths inimical. When the muirfowl rose before him, clangouring, he stopped with hands of twitching terror on his mantle; the whistle of a whaup would kindle gleams of searching apprehension in those orbits framed behind the velvet; sometimes a flock of wheeling plovers sent him skulking among bushes.

And yet the country and the morning were devoid of any visible hostility. No shapes of fear, no menace of conspiracy were in the glen. The river chattered friendlily; a thousand birds were warbling through the rain; the wild-flowers filled the air with the very breath of innocence; mankind might never have been there before him; the world of passion seemed remote.

But still, for Peden, it was in a vale of terror that he went, glowered on by things invisible;

that rap at dawn upon the shuttered window and the cry of yon distracted messenger had withered up his fortitude. He gibbered as he stumbled through the rushes, "A voice in Ramah! A voice in Ramah! Mirren weeping for her children!" No warbling birds, no opening flowers, no tang of the rain-wet heather made themselves apparent to his senses; all his being was surrendered to the wonder at his own miraculous prevision, and his panic fears of what at any moment might descend—the shouting troopers and that fiend their captain, wet at the hands with the blood of good John Brown.

At last he had to leave the river hollow and go over stones at Carpell Burn, where was no scrog or scrap of leafy shelter; and his heart appeared to fill his bosom when he stood revealed to miles of open moorland. He knew it as he knew his Book—Ayrs Moss, so melancholy to his foot-sore wandering youth, so much more mournful now that every wind upon it was a dirge for Richie Cameron, and the hills before him, brown and desolate, and hung with rags of vapour which had often been his friend. It was the land he called the Wilderness—bleak, mossy, patched with the ashen grey of withered heather. There was no crevice of these heights that had not harboured him, no secret hollow where he had not worshipped with the persecuted. Had it been night, though only with the guidance of the stars!—but daylight that was never favourite with him; and Claverse on the hunt, his skirmishers perhaps in every valley!

Oh, piteous Ayr, become a land oppressed! Its villages sat quaking; ever to be looked or listened for at dawn or nightfall, glinting scabbards and the sound of drums!

Some miles away, beyond the road to Stra'ven, in a solitude so absolute that time itself as well as tragedy might have overlooked it, stood a tenant house that in this dawn of May was pitiful to hear and to behold. For it had a voice—no chink of it but gushed a widow's lamentations and the grief of bairns, and the very thatch appeared to weep; the blinded windows spoke of some disaster. At intervals a dog, as one bereft, pawed at the fastened door, raised up his head and howled, and fancy might have credited the bleating lambs, penned on the brae-face, with forebodings. No morning smoke came from the chimney: eternal night and cold were seemingly come down on the home of the Christian Carrier.

Peden, having wound by devious ways in safety to the Dippal foot, with every step accompanied by false alarms, a challenge in each whistle of the Wilderness, each distant rock or solitary rowan-tree a horseman to his timid imagination, broke from the cover of the burn at last with tremulous hesitation, and ventured forth upon the level round the house of woe, which he had quitted earlier in the morning, warned by his eerie sense of things impending.

One glance about him gave his worst surmises confirmation. There were still upon the sodden turf the hoof-prints of the troopers; the white-washed gable wall was splashed with red; a clump of tansy where the martyr fell was flattened. Only one event was manifest in the sound of grief's surrender that arose from the interior where so often he had joined in psalms.

He stood upon the threshold, lifting up his voice, and cried, "Anathema! Maranatha! Woe to the beast that ascendeth out of the bottomless pit and maketh war on the saints, and on his head the name of blasphemy!"

Silence, the most profound, fell on the wailing household for a moment.

He looked about him furtively. In these few hours the place had taken on unwonted mournfulness; here evermore, it seemed, should be a frozen hearth: surely never played here children on the knoll, nor rose upon that grassy holm the Sabbath worship of God's remnant! But most of all 'twas fear he felt that Moses had let his hand go down and Amalek prevail; that even the Cloak of Darkness could not save him any longer from his enemy.

There was a clatter of the iron sneck; the door was opened, and the widow looked upon the prophet. Her form was as the fir-tree, tall and slender; like to the bud of ash her slackened hair; her visage hard as stone, which yesterday was filled with melting love for all mankind. No more tears from now for Mirren Weir! The fount of them was arid as a cinder; she scarcely seemed to know she had an infant at her breast. Behind her stood a weeping girl of ten, a woman from the Waterhead, and David Steel of Lesmahagow and his wife.

"Ye have come back!" exclaimed the widow. "I little thought when ye said the morn was dark as ye departed that it would bide sae dark indeed."

“John?” said the prophet, mumbling from behind his foolish craven mask. “Is he in from the hill?” And the lie that was in the futile question almost turned upon his throat.

“In from the hill, I’ll warrant ye!” quo’ she, with unimaginable bitterness. “Come ben for yourself and see him!”

“I knew it!” said he, with the triumph, hardly to be concealed, of one whose foresight had been justified. “I warned ye to have linen ready when I wed ye to him, and I said this morn was fearful,” and he put a foot within the doorway.

“Nay! nay!” the widow cried, with a clutch upon his cloak of darkness. “Who looks on the face of him that was my man, John Brown, daur look without a mask on him: he never flinched himsel’ to look on men or devils.”

With his cloak released, the velvet off his forehead, and his face revealed as weather-beaten, shorn, astringent, lit with eyes fanatical, old Peden stood at last beside the bed himself had slept in seven hours before. He lifted off the plaid and shuddered. Not sorrow was in his face, nor any hint of Christian resignation, but a squall of furious hate.

“Dogs! dogs!” he cried, and shook his fists. “They would harry the sheep-folds of Israel and track the Lord’s anointed like to hares upon the mountain! Where is the one city of refuge from their cruel fangs in all this land? Some Kedash of Napthali, Bezer or Ramoth-Gilead? A bloody end and terrible, O Lord, to that messan whalp, John Graham of Claverhouse! Let him die without the witness of the spirit, and his bones be turned to whistles. Ay! ay! thou son of Belial, death's door is only on the hasp for thee; I see thee on the heather, all thy wars accomplished, thy tack run out; 'twere well for thee had thou been born without a limb to hash and haggle at the saints! . . . Let us pray!"

He prayed with a great gale of the spirit as he stood beside the bed, and aye the widow looked at him as the tears streamed down his face, and aye the widow wondered at the Providence which would rob her of her man and spare this ranting atomy, with neither wife nor wean. His prayer seemed never-ending; the knees of her were sore upon the flagstones; the woman of the Waterhead took out the children, who again were started to their crying, terrified by Peden's fierce Apocalyptic gusts; the pair from Lesmahagow—decent bodies!—felt that unction pass into their souls emollient as butter. They groaned with pious fervour.

"And now we will praise God!" said the prophet when his prayer was done, and whipped from his mantle-neuk a book of psalms. Alone he chanted:—

"He in his pavilion shall
Me hide in evil days;
In secret of his tent me hide,
And on a rock me raise."

The voice of him in praise was like the wind in withered sedges, dry and thin, now lifting to a shrill and scrannel quavering, now lapsing to a husky dying fall, and aye the widow woman looked at him and saw no grief nor any fire of vengeance, but a gloating. Her heart, made raw by her disaster, was exceeding sensitive; it touched her to the quick to find him vain that his prognostications were fulfilled, rejoicing in the very horror of the crime as confirmation of the very worst that he had thought of Claverhouse; the sappier in his unction that himself was not the victim.

She raised no voice herself, but looked out at the window, and what she saw with any comprehension added to her misery. Already the day had taken on a shining visage and the heartless laverock rained his rapture from the heavens. But there was no hillock visible on which she had not seen John's figure sometime dark against the sky; no drain or dyke that did not speak his handiwork; the very grass had lost its old significance; were the mountains levelled in the night and the verdure of the land destroyed by fire from heaven, she could not have a sense more anguished of a world made desolate.

"How happened it?" old Peden asked.

"Is that not kent to ye?" she asked. "Perhaps had ye but bided with us, John had never sought the hill. But gang ye would at yon unco hour of morning, and his sleep was broken, and he went with a flaughter-spade for peats as soon as he had seen ye over Greenock Water. The horsemen came on him from Cairntable, and they drove him to this very door. . . . I stood there with his bairns! I stood there with his bairns! . . . 'You will take the Oath!' said Claverse, and the pistol in his hand. John looked at him without a quiver, and the children grat. He put his hand a moment on the head of Isobel, and said, 'No oath for me except against Socinian and Arminian error!' 'Then to your prayers!' said Satan; 'I will give you three short minutes!' . . . They shot him. He had on a shirt that I tucked at the sleeves this very morning! I stood there with his bairns, and they were greetin' bitterly. 'What think ye of your husband now, my woman?' Claverse asked me. 'I never thought so much of him as at this hour!' I answered, and I gathered up—I gathered up—— What garred ye go this morning? Did ye jalouse this thing that was in store for me?" She grasped the prophet by the coat lapel and stared into his eyes; the vanity of his reputed gift possessed him.

"I had," croaked he, "a vision of the night, and heard as in a dwaum the crack of hagbuts. Oh! that I were there with John and Richie!"

"Nay, nay!" cried she, "for these were men and perished for the Covenant, and Alexander Peden aye was lurking in the breckens! Ye kent the doom appointed, and ye fled without a word of warning!"

"Wheesht, Mirren, wheesht!" said the woman of Lesmahagow.

"That will I not!" cried Mirren Weir, with a loweing eye. "This man that is alive and hale and my man John stretched yonder, has helped to make mickle dule in Galloway and Ayrshire. From the Patmos of Holland and the sanctuary of the Bass, he and his kind have egged on better men to the Grassmarket gallows and the cane-brakes of Carolina. Oh, Peden! Peden! Ye have the gift of prophecy, but not the grace of God as my John had it, nor the spirit of a puddock. Ye might have told me! Ye might have told me! But no! ye fled without a word, and took my husband for convoy, and he was the one to perish."

"Woman!"—began the prophet.

"No more a woman!—a widow wronged!" she cried. "It's many a time ye marched, but ye never yet got to the battlefield. You, indeed, to talk of the sword of Jeroboam! With your velvet mask and your cloak of darkness, and your prospect-glass to scan the land before ye ever ventured from your den! Where were ye when the remnant were at Bothwell Brig and Rullion Green?—like a brock on the bield of the hill! Ye have denounced the Indulgences, and who, forsooth, so much indulged as Alexander Peden, in every cot house in Carrick, Kyle, or Cunningham, or skulking in Glendyne of Sanquhar, or the hills of Wanlockhead, or in the thickets of Loch Trool? I value not your gift a docken leaf! Oh, God! had ye but told me what this morning threatened! John Brown! John Brown!"

A discernible change came upon Peden's countenance; he blenched who was saffron-wan by nature, and fell a-trembling to find himself for once regarded with defiance and contempt.

"I never set up to be a man of war," quo' he.

"Wha winna march," said she, "should never blow the trumpet! There's my man deid!"

"To him," said the prophet, "are all the purchased and promised blessings!"

"But still-and-on he's deid, and I'm a living woman!" she protested. "Ye never lifted hand nor tongue to save him. The veil has been taken off my face, and I see you, Peden, for the fox you are, and the rock your habitation!"

Before the fury of her voice the prophet shrank. At last he gathered his cloak about him, placed the mask again upon his pallid countenance, and skipped through the cottage door. The hillside for the moment had no dread for him that was any greater than his terror of that searching tongue. He dropped below the level of the Priesthill dwelling, dedicate to woe, and sought with shambling steps the upper waters of the Nethan; the footprints of the troopers leading to the west made his return to Sorn a hazard. But ever his eye was on the hilltops, ever his ear alert for some halloo.

The Making of Tam o' Shanter

It was a dirty day in mid-November. The roads of Nithsdale, after weeks of rain, were fetlock-deep with mire, and the gauger's pony, ten parishes and two hundred miles of roads like these to her credit for the week, was very weary. If she smelt her oats at Ellisland, she did not show it in the usual way by the quickened pace and the eager shudder of the withers; she had fallen from a canter to a trot, from a trot to a walk. The steam rose from her flanks, and the flakes of froth were washed from off her neck by the rain that fell continuously; her head hung low. On treeless slopes, seen dimly against vague horizons on that weeping afternoon, or rising over sky-lines thinly fringed with starved, wild, haggard pines; or again in the scanty winter woods, the pony and her rider might have seemed to an observer, had there been one, like the last survivors of some hopeless sally in the endless fight of man against unconquerable wilds. Sometimes she turned a sad complaining eye upon her master when she felt his heel.

He was weary himself—sick-tired to the very soul! It was not altogether the weariness of the flesh, for once that day, for a too brief hour, he had been mighty. Back beyond Dunscore, he had had the idea for a song at the sight of a girl who smiled upon him from a wayside steading, and suddenly he had felt the old fond rapture; wakened and transported—not by the girl, for she was soon forgotten, but by that heady gush of song creation that tore through his brain at times, and made him feel eternal and gigantic. He had not found the words for the song beyond "Ae fond kiss and then we sever," but he had the sweet low wail of it somewhere in his head, and was content to give every pulse of his heart to the emotion that he knew from experience he should easily find the words for later on.

There and then he was not weary. There and then was he invincible, for to him without research had come the true divine elation, that exaltation of the soul he sometimes sought for in the bottom of a glass with old companions, only to find a coarser substitute. 'Twas then he knew he would not die, he could not die; that he was older than the hills, and would outlast them; that he had been admitted to the Secret; that he partook of God's delight in that ancient hour when He was happy, and in one evening filled the empty space with shining stars! The rare joy of his senses went to his very blood and bone, so that his limbs became like iron; he could have split the oak with Cyclop fingers, or hurled the boulders of the Nith over the Lowther Hills!

Now, in this miry afternoon, home-coming, an utter weariness possessed him; holding him in body less than in his spirit. Round him was a landscape that in summer and in sunshine always filled his mornings with a gladness to contemplate, but was now become most gloomy and portentous. The dripping little woods were full of creaking boughs and lawless shadows; the mist-wrapped braes, appearing so inimical and strange; the river so inhuman and so out of key with any mood of conflict, helpless, swirling to the Solway just because it must, without volition, as men swirl giddily through space and time—these fed the stark rebellion of his soul at the fate that mastered him. And he was come in sight of Ellisland, his farm. The place brought to his soul a pang as if the memory of an ancient sin had stung him. There it was, its steading bowered in trees, near the verge of the gravelly precipice that sank to the river's side, a poet's farm, God help him!—a visionary's choice, as if a man could harvest crops of shilfy-song or winnow a rent from evening sunshine!

Clarke, his ploughman, came ganting—suspicious sign!—from the barn to take in his horse. Burns put the reins in his hand and looked at him for a moment like a man that bursts with tidings.

"Did ye ever hear tell o' Sisyphus, Will?" said he, and the ploughman stared at his master.

"Man!" said he, "I think there used to be an auld packman wi' that by-name that gaed aboot Kirkmahoe when I was there——"

"Na, na, Will, that wasna my Sisyphus," said Burns. "Ye can aye let down a pack, and a pack's something wise-like, but Sisyphus was a king in Corinth, and now he is in Hell, for doom to push a bowlder o' stane for ever up a hill where it winna bide. There's a lot mair joyous recreations

I could think o' for a king, that ance was happy, and can mind, that still has all his faculties about him, and beholds, at his labour, the accursed truth. My God! My God!" The cry burst from him like a cry of Calvary, and over his fields he looked, his sodden cauldrife fields, so helplessly unprofitable, and at his cottage with its dripping thatch already rotting, and at his fowls that sheltered in the byre door. In his eyes flamed wild rebellion.

"The Globe at Dumfries again!" thought the ploughman, turning to lead in the mare.

Burns held him for a moment with his hand upon his sleeve. "Tell me this, Will," he demanded. "Are ye a contented man? Do ye sleep sound at nicht? Do ye mind auld things? Do ye ever think ye micht be better? Do ye see yoursel' the actual man ye are? Do ye meet wi' mony folk that understand ye? Have ye ever had but a glimpse o' a' the possible joys o' life, and seen them gaun by ye like Nith down there, wi' you stuck helpless on the bank?"

The questions poured forth from him in a spate; he stood with his plaid half-loosened, as eager in his manner as if his fate were in the answer.

"O, I'm no' complainin'," said the ploughman, whose mind had grasped but little of this fierce, bewildering catechism. "I'm no' complainin', I aye tak' my meat, and sleep like a peerie."

Burns looked in the broad red face with envy, his own pallid and drawn with inward pain.

"Ye're the lucky man!" said he, and then he

started, for from the cottage came an infant's cry—piteous, pathetic, the protest of the soul that is torn from heaven for a space of years to suffer trial. A myriad fresh emotions shook the gauger as he listened, and last of all a gush of tenderness.

"In wi' the meare!" he said, and slapped her kindly on the shoulders.

. . . .

Next day was Saturday. He stayed at home.

"What Sisyphus was this ye were haiverin' to Will Clarke about last nicht, Rab?" asked his wife. "He's been at Sisyphus a' this mornin', and jalousin' it's some new sang ye are makin'. I tell't him I never heard tell o' Sisyphus."

"And I wish to the Lord I had never heard tell o' him either, Jean," said Burns. "He's just a chiel in a book, that had a gey ill task to do, and did the best he could, but could never get it done, and kent he couldna."

"Are ye sure it was a man, Rab?" asked Jean Armour. "It's liker to have been his wife," and she started to rock the cradle, humming a country air.

Burns wrapped his plaid about him, for the day, though dry, was bitter cold. He went down before the house on a path that wound to a slip of holm, and walked by the river's bank, here overhung by trees. The melancholy of the night before was gone completely; the irrevocable past and Ellisland's cold, clammy acres—"the riddlings of the world"—were no longer like a black dog on his back; he was even in a mood to rejoice that after all he had made a poet's choice, if not a farmer's, when he picked on Ellisland. To his mind came a promise he had made to Grose the week before that he should write a poem about the Carrick witches.

Now, it was the way of Burns, when he would spur emotion to give truth and passion to his lines, to seek, not through his later years for the inspiration, but in those golden irrecoverable hours that seemed to have concluded with abruptness, when he turned his back upon the land of Ayr. Never in youth had he been, strictly speaking, happy; sordid needs and fierce rebellions; shame, ambition, inability, and pride, made, in these early times, the texture of his being, and weighing now with then, his intellect would have convinced him that his present state was vastly more enjoyable. But the heart, and not the head, was ever his adjudicator, and his heart invested certain transient hours by Doon with incommunicable grandeur, for no other reason than that there and then he had been innocent and young. All Kyle, in such reflections, was invested with a fond and pensive charm for whose surrender the most princely future could not make amends. He loved her very stones!

From Edinburgh parlours, Highland and Border wanderings, communion with his social and intellectual betters, he had nothing learned that was not his already when he walked behind the plough, and all the fervours, all the sweet illusions and enchantments which he gave a voice in song were harvested in Ayrshire.

Babbling river!—babbling Nith!—a fonder cry,

a sweeter chuckle on the stones was in old Doon whereto this water of Dumfries recalled him. As on many a night, awake, an exile, and remembering, he followed her again through all her courses, from the great dark muirland reservoir, by deep ravines and Castle Downans fairy dells, down into Alloway and the bay of Ayr. It was the sound of distant waters, and estranged, that sang through his imaginative ear this afternoon; the river Ayr herself swept through his retrospect—how blest was he to have been born upon her banks!

Old homes, each with a ghost of him yet tenanting its silence, still were standing where he left them, faithful to the streams he had deserted—Mount Oliphant, Lochlie, Mossgiel; and folk he knew who had been young with him, still breathed the native air.

Thus wrapped in the essential sentiment of youth and home from which the vivifying spirit of his music always came, he turned his inward gaze upon the earliest scene that had impressed his childhood eerilie—the ruin of Kirk Alloway, and in a flash beheld its possibilities for the thing he sought.

The old Kirkoswald legend, and the man of Shanter Farm! The story cried for more of fantasy and fun than it ever got in Mauchline taverns, and Douglas Graham was manifestly designed by Heaven to be its chief protagonist.

The sun, as it were in benediction on his essay, burst through the surf of clouds and poured illumination. Burns paced beside the river, muttering,

> "When chapmen billies leave the street,
> And drouthy neebors, neebors meet,
> As market days are wearing late—

By God I have it! It's the night and it's the weather, and the right lilt for a body startin' on an unco journey wi' nae convoy except a wheen o' witches. Mirk lanes and dreepin' thickets; glaur underfoot; an angry wife at hame; an awfu' lowe in the aisle of Alloway; the Brig o' Doon to cross, and Shanter seven miles awa!

> —market days are wearing late,
> And folks begin to tak' the gate,
> And we sit—

And we sit, and we sit—now what would we be sittin' daein'? Are ye there, Shanter? Ay, there ye are, auld Truepenny! What would ye be sittin' late for? Bowsing, of course!

> And we sit bowsing at the nappy,
> And getting fou and unco happy—

Rab, man! ye rascal, ye're fair started! If gaugin' was as easy!"

For hours he paced the sheltered holm attended by the shapes of men and fantasy created by his will. Below, the Nith went rushing to the Solway, in ignorance of the appointed end, but fearless. Green plovers wheeled and cried above his fields; when the sun was whelmed in clouds, the air was cold. But not for Burns, who, for his fever, loosed the grey plaid and gave his bosom to the wind. Tears came to him, and laughter; he fell on each fancy like a prize and clutched it till it took a shape in cadence and in rhyme; more often better blessed as are the noblest artists, thought and words were born together in his brain.

A hundred times he went back on the lines completed, sometimes to enrich or chasten, but his aim was rather to maintain the whole in tone, as clouds are, and the forests, the colours of bays and ships, the sounds of storm, the choiring of the cherubim. And his imagination the more surely mastered him at every repetition, so that he shivered when

> The wind blew as 'twould blawn its last,
> The rattling showers rose on the blast,
> The speedy gleams the darkness swallowed;
> Loud, deep and lang, the thunder bellowed.

He wept at his image of brevity of pleasure that

> —like the snaw, falls in the river,
> A moment white then lost for ever.

He saw before him

> —Doon pour all its floods,

and only for a moment woke to see that it was the Nith that thundered at the bend.

The sun was setting on the distant hills when the poet was done; a rookery went clanging home, and to his bosom flew content. To his mind came that great ease, that satisfaction which attends on inspiration met with open arms, not shunned for fear or indolence, nor for a second set aside until the work is done. 'Twas done! 'Twas good! He felt himself a king, and this was his golden hour. From the stuff of dreams, from the impalpable air, he had fashioned human characters, had made a little world of Scottish people with all their whims and humours, mystery and fears. Oh! he loved them, drunk or sober—he, their creator, he that wrought the miracle and brought them from the void. But more he joyed that he had, in their making, maintained the deeper, greater, more abiding thing—the Symbol, the essential soul that makes all that is great in the art of man a microcosm, a miniature of the world—the world that cries with vast night-deep and interstellar tragedies, and stuns to think on, yet is no bigger than a nut! Ellisland's cold bankrupt acres?—Bah! How little did they matter! The glimpses of what had seemed a Paradise—Edinburgh and Clarinda, and the parlours lost?—a fig for them! The narrow ways, the hard, poor years in front, the shrinking store of money?—what matter if he died a beggar, he had lived this hour!

He went back by the river side, and in where the cradle rocked.

"Jean," he said, "I have made a poem."

"Magic Casements"

In these days, now that folk are busy reading *Annals of the Parish*—and they might be worse engaged, indeed, a singularly taking book! I prize exceedingly the home-spun Irvine humour of it—I have had the fancy to relate a droll experience that befell me once, in which the author took a part. It was the first but not the only time I got a peep at what lies out beyond this tolbooth of the flesh, these iron bars of reason that encage us with our businesses, our dubious certainties, our poor, cramped, timorous senses nothing better than the brutes, and I got that glorious vision through a daft man's eyes. At least he would be so reputed. But me, I cannot think of him as daft, nay, rather with the stanchions and the fetters of the spirit broken, flying where he wist!

John Galt had come to Ayrshire on a jaunt, to call, as he professed, upon a cousin's man who had a lint-work in the Vennel here, but more, I think, to see the country and the folk he put into his books. He was a great big body of a man, with jet-black hair and melancholy eyes; and what was his diversion but to play the flute! 'Twas droll to me to think that this pock-marked and namely gentleman had one time been my closest school-companion, and had travelled round the world and seen a multitude of wonders; had written books, and yet was come to sit a night or two at my fireside and play a fife. It was the first time that I heard his own air, "Lochnagar."

A few of us about that period made a practice to go down and sit an hour or two ilk other evening in the skippers' room of old Macaskill's Black Whale Inn at the foot of the Quayhead Wynd. "About that period," says I; ah, sirse! I must allow it was a long one; all my cronies of the skippers' room have died since-syne. I have grown old there in the Black Whale Inn, sitting at nights and musing on the world—lost ships, lost men, strange ports, God's charity, and the stars. And often in the winter nights, when harboured towns are dreary, seeping-wet with rain and shivering with the gale, there come across the quays to me the creaking of the blocks, the clattering of capstans, wind whistling in the cordage, seamen's cries, the smells of timber and of spices. It vexes to the core to think that I have seen so little of the world! "All places that the eye of Heaven rests upon are, to the wise man, ports and happy havens." Ah! yes, but this poor harbour!—this poor inn!—this done old man!

It was the back-end of the year when Galt came to us; he could hardly get about the town for dirty weather, and the consolation of his flute, I think, was sorely needed, for he rarely had a chance to venture out of doors. There had been in his mind, I knew, a fine idea to go round his boyhood's scenes and make a harvest of a crop we never laboured much in Ayrshire—characters of men and women, seaport yarns and landward oddities, queer sayings, country words going out of vogue. But his crop at the hinder-end resolved itself just into what he got of native lore from me.

He would play the flute to ancient airs that kittled up my memory, and, fairly started, I would crack away like some pen-gun.

There was one night yonder that he seemed to think my stock was done of things rememberable. He sharped the keelavine with which he jotted down his memoranda, hummed and hawed, and at the last proposed that I should take him to some tavern.

"They're very low, John; very low," says I. "Just suitable for common bodies like myself, or, antrin whiles, a merchant skipper;" and my eye was on his broad-cloth coat,—a desperate stylish gentleman was Johnny!

"There's nothing low in life," said he, "but as we make it. You have done very well in the way of playing up to my gentility, with sitting here at night like some douce married man that never rang a tavern bell, but I prefer to ken the way ye live for ordinar;" and he chuckled. "There must be some old howff where bachelors convene."

I took him to the Black Whale Inn, down lanes that sluiced with water, and, as was to be expected on a night so wild, found nobody was in the skippers' room. We ordered in the rummers, sat for half an hour at most our lones beside a chaffer fire, and listened to the rain play blash upon the shutters. A scoury night, I'll warrant you!—and cold. We had not been long out of it when it drew on to sleet.

It came upon me of a sudden, sitting there, the pair of us, that we were two old men!

He was a namely character, and I had built a thriving business—but our youth was bye! I took at first a fright to think of it! So many things undone—so many joys untasted—loves no more open to me—visions drifted—voices changed! Could this be all that fortune had to give us at the last of it, to sit, two bodachs, drinking toddy by a tavern fire? Well might the young ones, having neither fame nor fortune, look on us with pity, still in the morning breeze themselves or walking in the moonlight, keeping tryst.

Perhaps it was a fancy, but I thought the same wae humour came to Galt. For once we had not much to say. He looked asklent at me, and then a long while in the fire, and then, in some queer wanton cantrip, put his flute together and began to play. Perhaps you know an air called "Bennachie"?—"Ae day gie me o' youthfu' life at the back o' Bennachie."

He breathed it very soft into the instrument; he chirmed it, as we say of linties whistling quietly with yon melancholy note they have before the storm. I took my toddy-ladle and I beat the time upon my knee; and out of doors the wind cried like a hopeless being minding happier things.

His verse was hardly finished when the chamber door went bang, and in upon us came a man for all the world like Aiken Drum. He had the clothing of a supercargo; something of the shipping line at least was in his sea-boots and his stunted jacket; but there surely never walked the poop more orra figure. His frame was like a tattie-bogle's, every joint a bulge below his soaking garments. Never a cap was on the creature; he was boulder-bald; a high wide cliff of forehead beetled over deep-sunk pits of eyes. The sleet was in his beard; he bore a book below his oxter.

Without a word for us at first he clapped down on a chair, syne pulled the hares-foot, summonsing Macaskill, and demanded ale. He took a draught of it, then turned on us as though we had been objects conjured by his mind.

"The night is wild," said he with great solemnity, "and it is far from Talavera!"

"Far, indeed, from Talavera, sir," I answered, "and indeed the night is wild."

John Galt said neither buff nor sty, but took apart his flute and stuck it in his pocket.

The stranger started at my words, as if a human voice was something he had not expected. He dragged his chair beside me, gripped me by the knee, and put his face so close to mine I felt the chill come off the sleet upon him. "Yes! Yes!" said he, "but further still from Avalon, and Trebizond, and Babylon, and I have been to Babylon and the night is wild!"

"I have never been, alas!" said I, "to Babylon."

My notion was to humour him: and yet he did not look like one debauched. At these high-sounding names the visage of John Galt was quickened. He gave a scrutinizing look, then out his keelavine!

"You have not been to Babylon!" the stranger cried, like one amazed. "Nor Trebizond, nor Samarcand, nor by the fable of Bellerus old! What! not Sargasso Sea nor yet in Nineveh! By heavens, the night is dark, and wild, and it is far from Talavera!"

He pushed away his flagon from him, drew his chair in to the table, took the book from underneath his arm and turned the leaves.

It was a book of poems and ballads.

The gutters of the quayhead lane were running with the gluck of burns; the tavern shook with every wave that burst upon the wharf; between the blasts we heard the seagull screaming in the dungeon of the mirk. There is a melancholy that I want the words for in such winter nights in small declining ports where fortunes have been made and lost; where ships have rotted for the lack of freight or sailed abroad with no returning; dead skippers in the graveyard, foreign shells on mantle-braces, grasses dried, and lava from Vesuvius; eggs of the ostrich, pouches made of the feet of the albatross——

"Drink up!" I bade him hurriedly. "Drink up, and have another measure!" but he paid no heed.

"Listen!" he said, with a kindled face, and placed the open book before him on the table with his head between his hands:

"The voice I hear this passing night was heard,
 In ancient days by emperor and clown:
Perhaps the self-same song that found a path
  Through the sad heart of Ruth, when, sick for home,
 She stood in tears amid the alien corn;
  The same that oft-times hath
Charmed magic casements, opening on the foam
 Of perilous seas, in fairy lands forlorn."

He read it like a man uplifted, with some fury of the heart; it moved me like a revelation, though I knew right well that noble stanza.

"You follow?—'Magic casements,' " he repeated, with a raised, indeed a frenzied eye. "And 'opening' you will notice, 'on the foam of perilous seas.' By God!—'of perilous seas'! Where are the perilous seas? I ask you.—'In fairy lands! In fairy lands forlorn!' "

He put his face upon the open book and burst in tears!

I looked at him with fellow-feeling—truly noble lines! Not Rab himself could better them. Forby that, I had just discovered I was old, and this that was revealed to me had something of the glamourie of youthful days. The sun, you thought, would never sink on such an ocean, nay, nor years impose a care! There must, I felt, be something in it! For our comfort! They were forlorn, these lands, because we did not beach upon them, tossed on the gurly wave in silly cobles. Oh! many a time, since-syne, I've got the same quick glisk—but for a moment—at the gleeful truth behind appearance. An Eastern name sometimes has brought it—from the lips of some rough sailor, or I've heard it whispered in the night-time by the night itself, or seen it on the water in the glitter of the moon.

The stranger checked the transport of his feelings, raised his head and spoke to me again. "Dark is the night," said he, "and far from Talavera! I have not been there, but it is in the land of Spain, and well I love the name, for why I cannot tell you. Should any one ask you, tell them all is dark in Talavera. Dark! Dark!"

I looked at Galt; his face was like a monument; upon my word he had not got a gleam of comprehension, fumbling with his pencil! It dawned upon me that he had his bounds!

"The man who wrote that, builded better than the Pyramids of Egypt!" I said to the stranger. "It always fills me with a something I could maybe play upon the flute if I was master of that instrument."

"He wrote in two lines there," cried out the stranger, "what has never been surpassed. And it is like the place. I've seen it! I roamed the world for it, and sailed what seas there are in search of it, and came at last upon it, after fever, in a place called Maracaibo, where we fought with buccaneers."

"What! you have seen it!" I cried, shaken.

"That, 'faith, have I!" he declared with pride, and the eyes of him like coals.

He had seen it! This windlestrae of a man with the cliff of skull and the raptured voice had seen the magic isle and open casements, on some day, perhaps, when I was busy with the things of Time!

"Sir," I said, "let us thank God! Sometimes I have wondered; I have doubted; I have feared. It seemed as if it could not really be. You must be a good man, since Heaven has shown you such high favour. At times I have thought, myself, to go out in search of it, for I was, one time, young, and had a brave spirit, and I have never had a home or lover. But the years passed—sirse! how the years passed! and I made a store of money——"

"Money!" said the stranger, wincing, and drew back from me. "It is very dark, and far from

Talavera! . . . Tell them, if they ask you, that her name was Isobella."

He gave the name so soft a turn, it mourned upon his tongue, and moved me like the owercome of a song.

I yearned unto him there and then, and longed to question him upon the maid that I might ken of her, but dared not speak her name.

"How gat ye there, sir ?" I inquired of him.

"I thought of it, and better thought of it," he said with great simplicity; "it was an isle, I knew—a cay perhaps of coral, very lonely on the sea, but all-sufficient. And there it never was but Spring and the sou'-west wind. The sea, I would be thinking, would come in and break in surf upon a creek of it where young folk would be sitting on the sands and sea-birds would be crying all day long. But there must be a home upon the isle, and lattice windows opening on the foam. . . . I will tell you—for you are old—the name of her was Isobella."

Again it sounded like a chime!

"It is a sweet name," I said. "For this gladness I will pray for all that bear it."

"I went on ships," said he, throwing back his head again, "and through the Maelstrom, and Sargasso Sea, and the Caribbean, and looked upon the islands of the ocean. There is Atlantis, and there is Avalon; Calypso's isle, and Hybrasail that is peculiarly for Erin and the people of the west, but none of them at all was of the magic casements. And then, one day, on a sea of peril, I saw sunlight glittering on lattice windows. It was a castle on the reef, and there I heard the harp of Isobella."

"Yes! yes!" I cried, "and then?"

He turned about and slyly put his book into his pocket, as another man, with sleet upon his clothing, and a stern official eye, came in and laid a hand upon his arm.

"You have found me!" said my friend. "I was on the point of going. Wild is the night and we are far from Talavera!"

. . . .

They went out in the night, the pair of them, abreast, and he that was the fugitive, stepped like a man enchanted. Methought it was not dripping pilot that he wore, but cloth of gold, and on the head of him a jewel. The steeple bell was clashing through the lift above the tenant lands; the sound of it came to me but in fragments—tattered rags of ringing, blown upon the storm; more close at hand, and clear within the harbour, I could hear the cry of one curlew. I stood bewildered in the skippers' room, forgetting that my other friend was there until he spoke to me.

"I thought for a little, yonder, I had got a story," said John Galt, and put away his keelavine and pocket-book.

"What! what!" cried I, amazed at him; "ye mean to tell me that ye didna!"

He had a face as set as flint, while I was nearly greeting.

"Tuts! nothing but the ravings o' a crazy man!" he said, and glowered at me.

"Oh Lord! and you to play the flute and work

at poetry!" I cried; and I was vexed for him. "Ah, John, ye write a bonny book, I'm no' denying, but I'm feared ye're still far ben within the bridewell o' the body. Or ye are older, far, than me. Or ye have been ower lang awa frae Scotland!"

The Democrat

The stores and arms of the smuggler's brig which the gauger Burns had boarded, sword in hand, on the previous day in the shallows of the Solway were being sold by auction in Dumfries. Cutlasses and brandy-kegs, muskets and marlin-spikes, were rapidly knocked down to peaceable burgesses who did not very much want them, but were rendered recklessly acquisitive by the humorous sallies of Jock Pender the auctioneer, who was using the smuggler skipper's pistol for a gavel, and kept a couple of men from Taylor's Inn going briskly round the crowd with copious supplies of spirits, ale, and cake.

"And now, gentlemen," said the auctioneer, "we come at last to the bulky stuff; thae four cannon—genuine Carron; see the mark o' the foundry on them for yoursel's. For a nice bit decoration to a house wi' a plot o' grun in front, there's naething beats a pair o' cannon. They're a' the vogue the now in London. There they are—thirty-two-pounders, scoops, sponges, rammers; mounted a' complete! I've never had a finer lot o' stuff gae through my hands. They're worth twenty pounds a-piece if they're worth a penny, but I'll no' ask that for them; wha bids five?"

"Shillin's," cried Willie Armstrong the persistent humorist, and Pender turned upon him with derision.

“Man, Will,” he said, “they’re worth that just to look at; what *you* want’s a pen-gun and a wheen peas to pap sparrows wi’. Come awa’ wi’ a wise-like offer.”

“What the deil would I dae wi’ them?” asked Armstrong, munching cake.

“Ye could stick them down before your door to frighten aff your creditors,” suggested the auctioneer, and the humorist withdrew discomfited to solace himself with draughts of eleemosynary ale.

Burns, who had never been to bed since he left the boarding party on the previous day, stood by the carronades with a foot upon a trunnion; a man with the heart to gush with tenderness for mouse or daisy ruined by his coulter, he yet had a love of arms, and kept upon his desk in the little closet in the Vennel the dirk of Balmerino. Arms were to him not cruel things for slaughtering, but the tools of valour, instruments of liberty, accoutrements of romance. Here they were, the carronades, grotesquely out of place in Pender’s yard; squat, dumpy, silent, gaping with open throats for the breath of war. Nobody made an offer. He searched the faces round him for a sign that any one experienced his feelings at the sight of the degraded guns—not beautiful in themselves, but for him evocative of a sentiment as keen as he could get from morions and hauberks; he saw indifference; the good folk of Dumfries looked on this ordnance as so much useless junk.

“Three pounds for the lot,” he rapped out, slapping his hand upon a muzzle.

"Thank ye, Mr. Burns!" said the auctioneer. "Three pounds I'm offered for the lot; ony advance on three pounds? Going—going—gone!" And he brought the pistol down on the head of a harness cask.

"Oh, the devil!" said Burns, taken aback to have his impetuous bid so soon accepted. "What am I to dae wi' a battery in the Vennel?"

"Ye can gie them to the French," suggested the auctioneer, and the face of the poet lightened.

"Faith I can!" said he. "Vive la Révolution! I'll pack them aff the morn's morn," and he met the astonished and reproachful gaze of Bailie M'Kie with amused defiance.

The sale went on; the Bailie sidled up to Burns on the outskirts of the crowd and set about a delicate remonstrance. He was perhaps the only man within the burgh qualified to do it without offence, for he came from Ayr, was old enough to have been once the poet's father's friend, and the poet and he, at many a Sunday skailin' of the kirk, cracked fondly about Carrick, both convinced it was the bonniest region in the realm of Scotland.

"I havena seen ye for a fortnight gane, Robert," he began, scooping up a pinch of snuff with a tiny ivory ladle. "I hear that besides chasin' the runners, ye've been at Mossgiel wi' your brother Gilbert. How's the mother?"

"Gettin' gey frail," said Burns sadly. "I went up ane's errand just to see her. Ye wouldna ken her, Bailie—crined awa to a shadow! But still the pride o' life and the vanity o' the eye in her, thank God! As particular about the piping o' her mutches as she ever was. Man, I wish I had her spunk!"

"Ah, dear me!" said the Bailie pensively. "I mind o' Agnes on her marriage day; she was a dashing one! H'm! we're a' gettin on in years. And what way's Gilbert? Is he keepin' fine?"

"Oh, Gilbert's strugglin' at it! Ye ken yoursel' what Mossgiel is?—a gey cauld clarty hole; there's nae fineness in't for ony tenant, no, nor in ony place in Ayrshire but for landlords."

"Yes, yes, I understand," said Bailie M'Kie. "Too true, Robert! Too true! But the market's risin'. And cauld and clarty, or no' cauld and clarty, I must say mysel' I aye liked Mossgiel."

"I'm like that myself about it," said the poet. "It broke my heart, God d—n it! but in these days I was free, and no' a slave o' Geordie's, rummaging auld women's cellars. Besides that, it was Ayrshire, and no' so many gutsy money-bags gaun on the Mauchline plainstanes as in this Dumfries. Did ye ever see a town wi' mair respect for Mammon or mair terror o' a man reputed to hae Whiggish sentiments? They're beginnin' to think that I have horns! Ye're magistrate o' a bonny toon, Bailie!"

Bailie M'Kie snuffed nervously. "About thae cannons, Robert," he remarked. "It's none o' my affair perhaps, but I ken't your folk and I have a great respect for ye, so I hope ye're no' in earnest about sendin' thae things to the French. The Supervisor would be sure to hear o't."

Burns shrugged his shoulders. "Bailie," said he, "I have nae doubt that he will; there's a lot o' sneck-drawers about Dumfries to clype a' my political indiscretions to Corbet, but I canna help it, I could never be discreet. I abominate the very word; it has a Hanoverian smell. I ken fine a' the Corbies o' Dumfries are down on me because they understand I'm Jacobin, because I said George Washington was a better man than Pitt—and so he is, a thousand times!—and because I read the *Gazetteer*."

"Whisht! that's a' right!" whispered the Bailie, with a timid glance around to see that they were not overheard. "I whiles read the *Gazetteer* mysel', and ye ken I'm as Whig as onything—in reason, Robert, in reason! but you're in the excise, drawin' your seventy pounds a year frae Geordie; ye should keep a calm sough and let independent men like Dr. Maxwell or John Syme rant sedition. Think what ye like, man, but keep your mouth steeked; that's my advice to you, Robert!" and again he drenched himself with maccabaw, and turned away with apprehension that some gentry from the outskirts of the burgh were regarding them suspiciously.

Burns seized him by the shoulder. "That's the real sneck-drawin' policy, Bailie," he said, "and I'm no' fit for it. The guns are gaun to France the morn's mornin':—

Heard ye o' the Tree o' France,
  And wot ye what's the name o't?
Around it a' the patriots dance,
  Weel Europe kens the fame o't.
It stands where ance the Bastille stood—
  A prison built by kings, man,
When Superstition's hellish brood
  Kept France in leading-strings, man."

He clung to the arm of the affrighted magistrate while he hummed the unholy verse, then released him with a laugh and went home for dinner.

Sure enough, the cannons went next morning with a letter from the poet to the French Convention. The fact was bruited round the town before the twelve-hours' dram. The merchant folk were dubious that the prank was rather daring even for a harum-scarum poet; the gentry of the burgh were disgusted. He felt that week a polar rigour in the air; his closest friends were desperately busy; they were not to be found even of an evening at the Globe. "It's silly! Downricht silly!" said M'Kie one evening to him, having risked a first-rate civic reputation, even the prospect of the Provost's chain, by sneaking in the dusk to the poet's domicile. "I warned ye it was rank sedition and worse than that, it was throwin' awa guid money, for it's no' to be expected that the French 'll get the guns."

"That's what I told him!" said Jean Armour. "Three pounds thrown awa on silly nonsense! But Rab's sae heidstrong!"

"Ye've made an awfu' hash o't, Robert," said the Bailie, "and ye're bound to hae Collector Mitchell down upon ye. Everybody's talkin' o' your rebel principles and sayin' ye're a dangerous man, prepared to see even Britain go to wreck and ruin. I ken better, bein' a Mauchline man, and what I thought was that ye might come up to-morrow night to the Masons' meetin' and set things right sae far as possible wi' a stave o' the patriotic."

"What kind o' stave?" the poet asked, smiling.

"Oh, ony kind o' trumpet stuff would serve for the occasion; ye could slap a couple o' stanzas up in half a jiffy; I would get them printed aff and circulated round."

"I daresay that!" said Burns. "Most kind of you! But I'm no' gaun to buy the gudewill o' Dumfries wi' patriotic stanzas made to order, Bailie, and your dainty bit plan would mak' me angry if it hadna got its comic side."

"Well, tak' my word for't, Robert," said the disappointed Bailie, "ye've made a bonny hash o' things, and may say 'fareweel' to the Friars Carse folk, Craigdarroch, Lawrie, and the ladies o' Woodley Park."

"Fareweel and fair-good-e'en to them if that be so!" said Burns with a flashing eye; "I may doff my hat to them at times but no' my politics."

Bailie M'Kie was right too; only the tradesmen and artisans—Pyats as they onetime called them—could remain his friends. As in defiance, his political demeanour grew more boldly individual as time went on, and one night in the theatre when "God save the King" was played he sat and kept his hat on. "Turn him out!" "Shame, Burns!" cried the loyal citizens. Next day he walked the street alone, shunned by all but a few reckless revolutionaries, regarded with eyes askance.

He clearly realised the situation; now the air was worse than polar, having a sepulchral chill. Men who were proud to be seen walking with him some months ago transparently jinked now into quite inappropriate shops when they saw him coming. The most illuminating evidence of the state of things was to be seen in the ridiculous alarm of Brown, the saddler, who, coming hurriedly out of his shop with his brattie on to seek refreshment in a tavern across the way, turned and fled back like a startled hen at the very sight of Burns, whom he had so often joined in a post-meridian dram.

"Brown, too!" said the poet to himself with bitterness. "Well, poor soul! he has to think of his Dalswinton customers! And I should hae a bell about my neck—a leper's bell to let a' respectable, canny merchant-bodies ken that I'm on the street."

One man crossed and spoke to him—young Grierson, whom once he had befriended in a smuggling affair, a fellow with no character to lose. "Ye're takin' the air, Mr. Burns?" he said politely, and the poet smiled a little ruefully.

"Ye see I'm welcome to as much of it as can be got on this side of the street," he said; "there's none of my fine friends over there inclined to share it." The ladies of Woodley Park and half a dozen lairds had that moment crossed the causeway to the other side with the obvious intention to avoid him.

"I thought ye were maybe makin' a sang," said Grierson sympathetically.

Burns shrugged his shoulders. "I got the drift o' ane to an auld air just now," he answered:—

> "Policy parts good company.

The honest folk o' Dumfries are a' content to tak' the shady side o' the street because a Republican rogue tak's the liberty o' strollin' in the sun."

"It's thae d—n guns o' yours!" explained young Grierson impetuously. "What way do ye no' deny ye ever sent them?"

"It would be a lee if I did," said Burns. "I have lee'd wi' a glass, and lee'd—God help me!—wi' a lass, but I canna, drunk or sober, lee about my heart's convictions. Well, *vogue la galère*!—and that's French for ye, Jamie—come on and hae a dram!"

"Over to the Inn?" said Grierson agreeably.

"Nay, nay, young James! nae inns for us to-day! Too many o' my friends are there. Do ye ken Grizzel Baillie's ballad?—

His bonnet stood ance fu' fair on his brow,
His auld ane looked better than mony ane's new;
But now he lets't wear ony way it will hing,
And casts himself dowie upon the corn bing.

O were we young, as we ance hae been,
We sud hae been galloping doun on yon green,
And linking it ower the lily-white lea,—
And werena my heart light I wad dee!

"Only my heart's no' light, James; that's where the ditty fails me. . . . Where in a' the world are thae folk crowdin'?"

"Then ye havena heard the news!" cried Grierson, astonished. "We're gaun to war wi' France; she threatens to invade us, and these are Volunteers. I joined mysel' an hour ago!"

. . . .

When Burns got home to his house in the Vennel, Jean, his wife, was baking scones.

"What's that on your hat?" said she; it had a bow of coloured ribbons.

"Great news!" he cried, elated. "The French are goin' to fight us, and I've joined the Volunteers. I wish to the Lord I had back my cannons!"

"Three pounds! And the children needin' boots! Ye're a braw poet, but there's whiles ye're awfu' stupid, Robert!" said Jean Armour. "And the French are goin' to fight us, are they? When are the puir deluded bodies goin' to start?"

"The sooner the better so far as I'm concerned," said Burns. "I'll be better wi' a gun than at the gaugin'. But the idiots up the toun imagine"—and he laughed—"that I'm no patriot!"

"If that's the case," said his wife as she cut the scones upon the griddle, "they canna hae read a great deal o' your poetry."

The Three Brothers

Having reached the spot whence Clashlet should be visible, and the very odour of its peats apparent, I stood among tufts of myrtle, and looked across the hollow country for at least a ruined gable of the steading. Not a single stone of it was to be seen! There was still the sheepfold down beside the burn, for the dry-stone shelters of the sheep persist long after the mortared homes of men have crumbled to the dust; and the rowan tree, with its berries reddening, was yet upon the knoll; but house, and barn, and byre, and garden had completely disappeared. It seemed incredible that this thing could have happened in the space of five-and-twenty years,—Clashlet's fires extinguished; the strong grey walls and oaken cabars swept from the surface of the earth as by a scythe; the household scattered to the void; the ordeal of Lily Armstrong ended. I went down the grass-obliterated, almost undistinguishable path, to find myself knee-deep in nettles upon what had been a threshold; of her tiny patch of garden naught remained but a clump of rank-grown tansy.

There were three brothers in Clashlet—one like a rock, and one like a larch, and one like running water. Their names were Dugald, Paul, and John, and I name them in order of their ages, Dugald being eldest. Of the three he had travelled farthest and seen most, having carried a draper's pack for years in the North of England, and come home to Clashlet on his father's death, to take command of three thousand black-faced sheep at a time when wool was at its highest. Short, thick, bow-legged, and powerful, with head and beard of a granite-grey, he seemed, in body, as in spirit, like a being hewn from stone.

His favourite word was "wrestling." "We must be wrestling!" would he say of a morning's clipping; of a bargain about tups; of the machinations of a personal Devil; of carnal appetites whereof he had his share. He wrestled without ceasing, not only against principalities and powers, but against all things tender, delicate, or beautiful. The very rose that Lily Armstrong tried to train against their porch aroused in him contemptuous opposition. And yet I must say a good man after his own fashion; a very monster of integrity, hating lies, incapable of mean evasions, ready to be ground to powder for the sake of any of the trivial convictions which he cherished as the inspirations of Omnipotence. Once on an autumn day he had walked fifty miles without a halt to restore a shilling, of which by miscalculation he had wronged a man at a Wigtown market.

Paul was like a larch that had rooted in a crevice of that cliff, his elder brother. Situated elsewhere, free from that tyrannic influence, timeously relieved from his allegiance to the family Capital and the family ties, he might, I think, have been a splendid man. He had 'listed once at a Fair; and the sergeant, measuring his six-feet-three, had mentally marked him for the Guards, but Dugald on the morrow wrenched his brother from this appropriate destiny, and took him home to Clashlet in a cart.

"Ye must wrestle, Paul," said he, "against the pomps of redcoats and of trumpets; God made ye for the hill!"

So the sapling Paul thereafter herded the sheep they had inherited, relinquishing a dream of independence and adventure, his head high in the air, but his feet imprisoned by the fraternal rock.

Finally there was John the instable, irresolute as the weather-vane, fluid as Clashlet Burn. Through him, directly, came the tragedy. They say, who knew him best, that he was a man of good intentions; that he was unselfish; that he would not hurt a fly; it is the subtlety of Nature that she should make the immediate instruments of her cruelty so often of such seeming harmless creatures. Dugald may be absolved hereafter, being a man of stone from his nativity, insensible of what he did; Paul may come through that last Assize assoilyied and admonished, as a passive agent in that poor girl's ruin, being under dominance of his elder brother. But the deepest pit and all the torments of eternity would not be expiation for the sin of John, who, capable of loving Lily Armstrong, was likewise capable of standing timorous and acquiescent while the gentle creature perished in the clayey furrows of Clashlet Farm.

The domestic tragedy of the taunt, the blow, yea, even the knife or pistol, is less atrocious than that whereof she was the victim, yet was it witnessed going on for years by a country-side that offered no intervention. For the case of Lily Armstrong is commonplace; such women's tragedies are enacted in every rural parish. But to me, who had seen the same sad fate in other instances and must remain inactive, things being as they are and wives but chattels, there were features of this wretched woman's case that rendered it peculiarly lurid and appalling. Seeing her in church attended by the brothers—she, pale and woebegone and disillusioned, each year more shabby of attire, less scrupulous of appearance, manifestly sinking deeper every season in the slough, my heart was torn to think of what she used to be and what she might have been. Ah! child of sorrow, had I known thee in the days when I was young and thou wert still unbroken! . . .

When the mother of the three men died it was Dugald who said, "We need a woman-body here in Clashlet; wool is going down; we cannot afford or depend on housekeepers; you, John, better cast an eye about for a good strong wife." The youngest brother took his counsel. He found himself, at one time, at a Cattle Show in a distant part of the country, where the daughter of a widowed innkeeper, impressed, as women will be, by some superficial graces and the prospect of an Arcadian life in a farm of three thousand sheep, fell in love with him, and came home with him his wife.

The sight of her, on her coming home, astonished us; she was so utterly incongruous with Clashlet and its tenants. A town girl—nay, a town lady; well-bred, refined, and elegant; you saw it in her dress and carriage, even before you saw it in the radiant alertness of her eye, the sensitive and mobile face, or heard it in the cultivated accents of her melodious voice. Body and mind, she seemed without a blemish. In her presence her husband, John, whose figure and address were not amiss in a bucolic way, had the look of an awkward lout; the brothers, tailing in behind her to the church on that first Sunday of the tragedy, appeared like menials humbly attendant on a queen. Your heart went out to her! She bore, in her immediate presence, wizard powers to rouse and purify; our rural world seemed made to be her footstool.

That day her fascination culminated in her singing, which, without predominance of pitch or volume, welling from sincere ecstatic sources, gave to our psalmody the quality of vespers heard from dewy thickets. It seemed to us that one so rare and gifted must completely alter all that was sordid, ugly, mean, and calculating in the Clashlet house. But, the flower has only a fleeting season; the rock prevails; the larch upsprung from the cleft of it will wave its pennants in the sky for generations, and the water, howbeit shallow in its courses, suffers really nothing from drought or frost, but freshly glints and babbles again when the rigours are gone that ruin tranquil gardens.

"What was yon bowed head on the book-board for? We're not accustomed here to such Papistical play-acting!" said the elder brother to her when the service ended. "Too much of the concert in your singing too!"

She must have been appalled when she found to what a fate she was indentured! The wealth of Clashlet, of which her John had been so eloquent, was all upon the hill, and sedulously guarded by the brothers and their dogs; and, lessening in volume by each fall in prices, made its owners more and more niggard of the simplest comforts of the home. For them—for the rock especially—the family Capital, that must be kept intact, was everything; domestic pleasures were effeminate and sinful. Toiling like serfs themselves, they looked to Lily Armstrong for the unremitting labours of a slave and for a slave's subservience. She, who could be marvellously adorned by the simplest clothing of her choice, must forego the purchase of a single ribbon. Those few accomplishments her folk had paid for—the piano, singing, embroidery, a taste in books—would seem preposterously ludicrous practised by a wife with cows to milk at dawn, rough food to cook, turnips to single, hay to coil, mash to make, soiled clothes to wash, and stalls to clean. No servant had ever stayed in Clashlet long before her coming; the brothers were too terrible, the routine of that unlovely household was so overwhelming, and she, who yearned for some companionship, even though it were a slattern's, could not retain one but for the briefest period, even by her most excessive kindness. All fled from Clashlet after a short experience of that life from which she, being bond, could not escape.

It was not without a struggle that she sank; for

a time she strove to keep her head above that stagnant marsh of vile materialism,—to smile, to sing a little, nourish flowers, and seek communion with a few congenial souls who pitied and understood; but her destiny crushed her down. They broke the heart of her! They broke her pride! They might as well have stuffed the divot in her mouth!

Could we but see the degradation of a radiant spirit in the rapid movement of a cinematograph, the spectacle would horrify. I witnessed it extending over twenty years; and even thus deliberately beheld, it was a thing to make the hills round Clashlet dreadful as a dungeon's walls, the clangour of the burn as sinister to the ear as clanking shackles. Times bettered for the farmer; the partner brothers prospered, and greatly she helped their prospering, but it made no difference to Lily Armstrong, wife of a man of water, and slave to him and to his brothers, rock and pine.

Her brutal, unbefitting labours were no less essential to the men whose God was the family Capital. You could almost see her coarsening week by week; you saw, at least, the gradual hardening of that once sweet mouth, the dulling of that keen, glad eye; lost grace of movement, self-respect evanishing. Infected, as it were, by that miasmic atmosphere of gross materialism in which her days were spent, she, too, grew harsh, penurious, distrustful, and unlovely who had one time been a flower diffusing fragrance, generous as the rain, confiding, unaffected, frank, and capable of any sacrifice for love.

Thank God, no children came to the degraded

years of her who should, with a happier destiny, have mothered noble sons! She died on the verge of forty, prematurely aged and broken—heart and body; and her husband, who had always had some glimmering of the truth, wept maudlin tears upon her grave. She died a sacrifice to the family Capital—to three thousand black-faced sheep; and I rejoice to-day that there are no sheep of theirs on Clashlet nor a stone of its steading standing. Far better the deer—far better the wolf itself—on the hill of Clashlet than those creatures that maintained the only passion of the men who murdered Lily Armstrong!

Miss Jean

My first memory of Miss Jean is of a nimble little body, and a head wrapped monstrously in shawls. It was said that she sometimes wore as many as six of these shawls, one above the other, beginning with two in the hottest days of summer, and adding to them as the seasons passed and the days perceptibly grew less warm, till the first frost of winter came, when she covered all with the sixth, that was, unless my memory misleads me, of the tartan of Rob Roy. As she tripped about her parlour-room in Whitton's Close in a joyous haste to make me jelly pieces, she was my notion of a Brownie, that in every tale of the Highland nurse who reared me, is of no discoverable age, and small and kindly, its head a mystery, its footsteps hushed and agile. 'Twas herself, indeed, that gave me many a tale of Brownie and dwarf, never tiring to tell me of that fine world of fancy in stormy days when the window-panes were blurred with rain and sea-spray, so that she could not indulge her passion for looking out upon the Craig, the quay, the distant isles where lights flashed in the dusk.

Between the whiteness of her hair, as sometimes I was privileged to see it, and the agility of her footsteps; between the antiquity of her clothing, and the girlishness of her laugh and conversation, there was a disagreement that left me always dubious whether she was young or old; and her face that was smooth as wax, and her eyes that were like peat-hag pools in glints of sun, gave me no help to solve a puzzle that in truth quickly ceased to exercise my mind.

It was long after, when I learned that she had not set foot outside her own doors but once in more than forty years, nor had more fresh air been permitted to intrude upon her parlour solitude than came in unbidden when the door was opened for her to cry down to her maid, Katherine-Ann, to be sure and make herself a good dinner because the day was cold, and send a bowl of soup to each of the neediest neighbours in the Vennel.

Forty years!—it is a long time of hermitage, and on the verge of crying seas, and they so often dreadful! Once I remember, greatly daring, I proposed to take her out and show her a nest with young things in it, in our garden, and somehow the notion caught her fancy so that she had her feet upon the threshold. But there she paused and sighed, looking fearfully up and down the front of the deserted Land.

"Oh, how cold it is, little boy!" said she, shivering, though the air had the bland caress of June. "I will—I will go some other day, dear, when the weather is more kind!" And though I hung eagerly upon her gown, and tried to force her to my nestlings, she went in again, just faintly scolding me for my importunity.

In those days I did not know how it happened that Miss Jean was unlike the world, as my own people used to say of her. And I did not care. It would not have surprised me if I had been told of her long imprisonment in her parlour-room, that had been broken but the once on a night when—long before I was born—having heard of the Captain's new shandry-dan, she had been tempted by the last spasm of her woman's curiosity to go out with a lantern behind the sheds and look at this strange chariot. She had been followed by her maid, Katherine-Ann, who found her all trembling with pleasure at the splendour of the thing, and concealing a bright new crown-piece under the cushions for luck to the owner.

"Katherine-Ann, my dear," said she, "you will not tell the Captain or he will think me daft. It will please the good man to have an omen."

But, to come to what I learned long afterwards, Miss Jean's devotion to her fireside started with the loss of her sister Leevie. They were twins and orphans, the gayest of the gay, and—as I well believe it—old folks said they had been beautiful by-ordinary, loving one another so that the neighbours laughed at them—and loved each other better, too, because of the example. It was the time of the big old wars. Drums rolled in Ayr and Girvan, a soldier came and loved—or made pretence to—and marched at the last of it, behind his company, with poor Leevie crouched in shameful hiding in the bottom of a sutler's cart.

For days—for weeks—the house in Whitton's Close rang hideously with the name of Leevie who would never again come home to true love. And Miss Jean went out no more. She sat solitary in her parlour-room, the world for her at a standstill, the airs of heaven growing more unwelcome every year, her shawls more numerous, her face more waxen. No one from the outside world saw her except on New Year's days.

"It is so long since I have been over the door," she would say; "it must be a week at least, and I cannot bear to have the people asking for me and shaking hands. And besides, it is so cold!"

As for my intrusion on this strange solitary in Whitton's Close, it happened on a Hallowe'en. With other boys I had set out to the robbing of her tiny slip of garden, and had been caught by the maid, Katherine-Ann, and brought in terrified to face the woman with the shawls.

"Oh, dear!" she cried, half-weeping herself, and tripping round the room to seek for ha'pence and the guava jelly that came from some relative in distant parts. "Oh, dear! is not this the foolish boy to be frightened for Miss Jean that is just daft with liking for the young and venturesome! You may come and rob my garden every night till there is not a kale-stock left in it; though what a boy should want with kale-stocks on a Hallowe'en——"

And there she was feeding me—herself laughing girlishly the while—with great spoons of the marvellous jelly I learned to prize later, for its travels and its flavour of tropic isles. That and her tales brought me often back to her parlour, for all my fears of that swathed head and waxen face and piercing eyes. She was not like the world, as they must be whispering at home, but she had a heart of gold. All that sweet rare womanhood crystalled in one fine quality—kindness; she had a crave for the pleasure of doing generous deeds. The window of her parlour-room, as I have said, looked on the Craig, and Arran hills; but more closely it glanced upon the harbour, and the quay where throbs the life of our little community. Time stood for her, poor dear! Perhaps in some deep wisdom that we sane have not the secret of, she knew there is no space nor time nor death; but the hardships of poverty and age hurt her always to her tears. A going-about body passing the Land in a ragged coat almost made her open her window to cry him in; instead she would send Katherine-Ann after him with food. A woman standing in the cold on the quay waiting the return of her husband's skiff never failed to send her to the pomade-bottle that was her curious poor's-box. I have often seen her shake it gleefully between her and the light of the window, and cry, "Mercy on me! how the money goes! But what a merry sound!" And the coins would jingle a little in the bottle and then come tumbling into her palm, which was so small and plump that no coin could stay there long under any circumstances.

I think these days in Miss Jean's parlour were the happiest of my life; at least they were the best, the purest, the most profitable. What I heard and saw there lasts with me more memorable than anything I have heard or seen in the years of my manhood. And that is why I can mind of a New Year's Day when something happened in Miss Jean's in Whitton's Close that I did not understand, but is now as plain to me as if I read it in a story.

The New Year's Day, I have said, was the only

occasion of her contact with the outside world. A few friends—mostly old folks—made it a custom to put on their best and youthfullest, and come on that day to the parlour-room and wish Miss Jean the compliments of the season. It is later knowledge to me that there was an understanding among them, perhaps never mentioned but grown of itself in those good and thoughtful hearts who sought to save this over-grieved little lady fresh trials, that her impressions of how things stood in the outer world should suffer no correction; that for her the old should still be young as when she used to mingle with them; the long-dead still be quick and busy. But I did not know this as I sat that day in a lug-chair in Miss Jean's room, reading *The Holy War.* Her shawls for once were off; her hair, that was blanched to snow, was braided; she had a gown of blue silk, and all trembling with pleasure and excitement she busied herself in preparations among cordials and cakes and green tea, with now and then a turn to an ancient jar full of withered rose-leaves that she tossed in her fingers so that they might give a perfume to the room.

"Little boy," said she, "here's the garden still, but never a drop of dew."

The first of her visitors was an old lady she called Miss Marget, but who to me and all who moved outside that parlour-room was known as the Skipper's Widow. She was as round as a girr, had a face all crinkled with smiling, and kept on her mittens to conceal her marriage-ring as she sipped her claret-wine with an awkward unpractised youthfulness.

"Dear me, Miss Jean, it's you that's looking well!" said she, and glanced uneasily at me.

Miss Jean's face took on a glow that almost justified the flattery.

"You are a daft creature, Marget," said she, "and will never be wiser till you get a man." She laughed slyly, pushed her friend on the shoulder playfully, and "Is it still the Skipper?" said she.

"God be about us!" said the Skipper's Widow, and glanced again at me.

"And, oh dear, I'm wearied of waiting for Leevie and her husband!" said Miss Jean.

"There is no word of them coming this way soon, is there?" asked the Skipper's Widow, nibbling her cake and looking oddly out at the window with more than her usual colour in her cheeks.

"I expect they will be up here on Han'sel Monday," said Miss Jean. "They are to set up house in the town, for the Major must leave the Army, that is no place for a man with a wife and family."

"Oh, Aunty Jean! Aunty Jean!" cried the Skipper's Widow, laughing slyly, and Miss Jean blushed once more and pushed her gently on the arm again, and thrust more cake on her attention.

"Indeed, and I am very fond of bairns," said she, putting a hand for a moment on my head.

The Widow changed the topic, and entered eagerly upon discourse on dances and kirns, and marriages; and the odd thing to me was that she spoke of many names I could see on any Sunday carved under mort-head and cherubim in Girvan churchyard. It seemed to me that the play of old folks had some curious features, though Miss Jean Kennedy enjoyed it vastly, and the Widow must laugh determinedly, yet, as I noticed, always with an aim to keep the conversation as far away as could be from Miss Leevie. But to that topic Miss Jean as eagerly returned.

"Do you know, Marget," she cried, "what is troubling me is that Leevie and her man will find it ill to get a suitable house."

The Skipper's Widow gathered the crumbs in her lap, and made to shake them into the fireplace. To do so she must pass close to me as I sat in the lug-chair, and I noticed with some wonder that she was screwing up her eyes to keep back tears. Next moment she was turned about and bravely smiling.

"I was thinking of going about to look for a suitable place for them," said Miss Jean; "but I have not been over the door since—since Saturday."

"Indeed and I have not been seeing you going about," said the Skipper's Widow. "But there is plenty of time between now and Han'sel Monday."

When she was leaving, she said, "Be sure and call, my dear, when you are down the street," which Miss Jean, self-condemned to life's imprisonment, promised cheerfully to do.

It was something like this with all her New Year's visitors. They were all, it seemed, in a pact to keep the world youthful, and their old intimates immortal, and discourage, as well as they could, all reference to Miss Leevie. The most wonderful of all of them was the last, a gentleman whose by-name is vivid in my memory, and that she called him John, but whose surname I forget, if I ever knew it. I fear he had been at many hospitable houses before he reached Miss Jean's. I remember his roving eyes, his old-fashioned brass-buttoned coat, his red face, his uneasy laugh. She met him with a hand on each of his coat lapels.

"I was sure you would not forget us to-day," said she tenderly; and with something of discretion pressed on him a cup of her green tea, which he took with protestations of pleasure, but with more friendly glances towards her decanter.

"Forget!" said he. "Could the sea forget the shore, Miss Jean Kennedy? Tell me that!" and flourished the cup with the movement of one that gives a toast.

She was red with pleasure—this little woman with blanched hair and waxen face.

This time it was she who did not care to speak of Leevie, though the name would come in spite of her to her lips, to be checked there with a shamed expression.

"When Leevie comes, John—oh, I hope you are keeping quite well in this cold weather!"

He laughed loudly at this, though it seemed to me not with much sincerity.

"I never was a day ill in my life, Miss Jean," said he.

She put up protesting hands. "Hush, hush, John," she cried, glancing about her; "do not say that for fear God should hear you. I was once without trouble myself, and could not keep my heart low and humble in my hands, but must have it leaping high and vaunting, and then Leevie—you will take some sweet cake, John?"

"Anything that these fair hands have made," said that odd elderly gallant, as if she were a girl.

"Ah, John!" said she, "it was always the pretty speech with you. And—what was I going to say now? Oh yes, I am sorry, I am so sorry!"

She paused and looked pityingly at him.

He coughed; his brow was in a perspiration. I think he was not happy.

"I am so sorry Leevie treated you so badly, John," and she wrung her hands in distress, tears in her eyes.

"It does not matter; it really does not matter anything at all, Miss Jean," said he, and crumbled down the fragments of his cake upon the table. "It really does not matter much. I'm heart-whole, I assure you, except when I see her sister. Ha! ha! what do you think of that, Miss Jean? Except when I see her sister." And then he gave another flourish with his cup, an aged, awkward gallant, looking the while suspiciously at me, as if he feared my laughter.

"I know she—she—I know she liked you, John," said Miss Jean.

"Not a bit, not a bit!" said he quickly.

"Oh yes, she did that."

"Well, perhaps," he conceded; "but it went no further than just liking. What does it matter now anyway, poor girl!"

"I am glad you are not thinking of it," said Miss Jean more cheerfully, and made to fill another cup of tea. "After all, you have youth and the world before you yet, and there's as good fish in the sea as ever came out of it. We must just be glad our dear Leevie has made so good a match of it; the Major comes of a good family."

And at that the man with the by-name, whom she called John, gave a strange cry, put down his cup untasted, and ran ridiculously from the parlour-room.

"Come back this minute, John!" cried my dear friend, following him to the stair-landing, but he never turned.

Miss Jean came back to the room, not greatly distressed at this discourtesy. "Poor John," said she; "he takes a glass at the New Year. It was not like the thing at all between him and Leevie, not like the thing at all, and I'm glad he takes it so light-hearted."

It was by this time, I remember, late in the afternoon, and snow was falling. I had got to the window and looked at sea-gulls standing in a row upon the net-poles; on the idle boats lying along the wall; on Ailsa growing dim. The maid, Katherine-Ann, brought in hot water; Miss Jean washed the tea-dishes at the table, and I was thinking hard.

"Who was Leevie?" I asked, plunging to the mystery's core.

She smiled.

"Leevie is just my sister Olivia, my dear," said she; "Olivia Shaw, the Major's lady, and a bonnie lass she is, as you will see at her home-coming."

"Olivia," said I. "And Leevie is just Olivia. I did

not know. There is an Olivia Kennedy buried in the churchyard."

"Olivia Kennedy," she cried at that, her face all storm, her eyes alarmed, and she caught me by the arm. "What nonsense is this you are telling me, little boy? There never was but one Olivia in the parish—my dear sister that is now the Major's wife and will come home on Han'sel Monday. Oh, dear! it is so cold, I'm just shivering," and she started to put on her shawls, once more the Brownie.

Passing the kirkyard on my way home I looked over the dyke at the plot they call the Strangers' Ground. I was quite right in what I told Miss Jean; there was a slate-stone there, a generation old, and a little bit ajee, and cut on it the words:—

In Memory of
OLIVIA KENNEDY

Daughter of the late George Kennedy, Portioner in Dalmannoch,
Who died in Edinburgh, 3rd June 18—
Aged 19 years. And is interred here.

I spoke about the thing that night to my mother, who was much disturbed, and set me angrily to my lessons, though it was a time of holiday. And but for a promise that I should never name Leevie or Olivia to Miss Jean again, I would never have got back to the parlour in Whitton's Land.

like the wind in
withered sedges
shrill and scrannel
quavering
spirit of a puddock
a broken leaf
with shambling
steps
bowered in trees
cauldrife
the sun was whelmed
in the clouds
he joyed
it vexes to the core
in some queer unwitting
carking
orra

loud-roaring through
deep chasms overhung
with foliage & moss

the disease of lull contentment
uplift to the soul

with all his thoughts
insurgent against slumber

no breath of air was stirring
in the trees

repining
I'm sweir to break their
sleep

fog was thick upon the
coloured fields

vague forms arose like
sleepers

the river ran rolling through
the bouldered
fleets

looks to find words

Lightning Source UK Ltd.
Milton Keynes UK
21 March 2011

169613UK00001B/102/A

9 781843 500797